**'You don't h
out to attract
against the sn
her hair.**

'You're as enticing in the clumsy gear we wear
for work as in this beautiful dress.'

'So?' she challenged.

'So this,' he said softly, and like a thirsty man
who'd found an oasis he bent his mouth to hers
and kissed her.

His lips were firm and warm…and demanding.
His arms were where she wanted them to be—
around her.

This is it! Zoey thought dizzily.

Abigail Gordon loves to write about the fascinating combination of medicine and romance from her home in a Cheshire village. She is active in local affairs and is even called upon to write the script for the annual village pantomime!

Her eldest son is a hospital manager and helps with all her medical research. As part of a close-knit family, she treasures having two of her sons living close by and the third one not too far away. This also gives her the added pleasure of being able to watch her delightful grandchildren growing up.

Recent titles by the same author:

PARAMEDIC PARTNERS
EMERGENCY RESCUE
THE NURSE'S CHALLENGE

FIRE RESCUE

BY
ABIGAIL GORDON

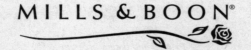

MILLS & BOON®

With grateful thanks to the men of Marple Fire Station

First published in Great Britain 2003
Harlequin Mills & Boon Limited,
Eton House, 18-24 Paradise Road, Richmond, Surrey TW9 1SR

© Abigail Gordon 2003

ISBN 0 263 83420 4

Set in Times Roman 10½ on 12 pt.
03-0103-48097

Printed and bound in Spain
by Litografia Rosés, S.A., Barcelona

CHAPTER ONE

ZOEY eyed the man in charge dubiously when he heaved himself out of the removal van. He was overweight, florid of face and wouldn't see sixty again.

His companion was a youth with a vacant face, spiked hair and an earring, which increased rather than detracted from her uneasy lack of confidence in the one-man firm that she'd employed to transport her belongings from a studio flat in the city to a more superior residence in the countryside.

But they seemed to be managing all right with a lot of puffing and panting from the big guy, and soon she was locking her door and preparing to follow the van to pastures new.

Pastures new in more ways than one, and her spirits were at their lowest.

Normally bright and bouncy, Zoey Lawrence had asked to be transferred from the job she loved in the bustling city to the quieter confines of a rural fire station.

Twelve months ago she would have scoffed at the idea, but life with its twists and turns had changed all that.

First of all there'd been the finish of her relationship with Damien. Damien the smiling charmer. A firefighter colleague who'd told her he loved her, while all the time he'd been doing the rounds of some of the young and attractive teachers they'd met during talks on fire safety in the schools.

She'd given the impression that she didn't care when

she'd ended the affair, but his deceit had hurt…a lot…and having to carry on working with him hadn't been easy. Especially as he'd been acting as if he'd been the injured party. She'd vowed grimly that another time she would be more wary of smiles and soft talk.

But that hadn't been the end of it. There had been worse misery to come…much worse…and it had made the break-up with Damien seem like just a passing cloud.

Two years ago her widower father had taken himself a new young wife and a few months ago they'd had a child. But sadly, with the baby only a few weeks old, he had collapsed and died from an embolism, leaving mother and baby to fend for themselves.

But Zoey had soon found that hadn't been happening. Mandy hadn't been coping at all. She'd spent the days bemoaning her loss and doing little else and Zoey had found herself going backwards and forwards between her job and Mandy's house like a yo-yo, offering comfort and making sure that baby Rosie wasn't being neglected.

It had all become too much and now she was about to move in with Mandy and the baby, while at the same time pursuing her career as a trauma technician in the fire service at a much smaller station than where she'd been employed before.

She was having to put her own life on hold because of the needs of her young stepmother and was happy to do it for her father's sake as much as anything, but sometimes she wondered where it would all end.

During the last traumatic weeks there hadn't been a moment to call her own, and as she followed the removal van in the Nissan Micra that had transported her from town to country so many times the future didn't look exactly bright.

*   *   *

They had arrived. Mandy was at the gate to greet them with a grizzling Rosie in her arms, and as Zoey reached out for her tiny stepsister she eyed Mandy's pale face.

'How are you?' she asked.

'Feeling better now you're here,' she replied tonelessly.

'Good,' Zoey told her bracingly as she cuddled the baby, adding with a vestige of the smile that could have charmed ducks out of the water when she was on top form, 'We're going to be just fine...the three of us. You'll see.'

The man had unlocked the van and he and his assistant were lifting out her wardrobe when the youth suddenly yelled, 'The boss ain't well, miss!'

As Zoey turned round she saw the wardrobe tilt forward, and as the lad frantically held onto it his companion slowly sank to the ground, clutching at his chest as he did so.

Passing Rosie quickly back to her mother, Zoey raced down the path and took the other end of the wardrobe to prevent it falling on the man. When they'd righted it she dropped down beside him and loosened his collar.

His skin was clammy, his breathing shallow, and the amount of chest pain he was experiencing indicated a heart attack.

Then she was racing past a dumbstruck Mandy to phone for an ambulance, giving the voice at the other end precise details of the man's condition and where he was to be found.

As she ran back to him Zoey saw that a car had stopped at the house facing Mandy's and a man was getting out of it. Would he come across to help? she wondered as she checked her patient's pulse.

Yet it would make no odds if he did. She knew what she was doing. It was vital that the patient was taken into Coronary Care as soon as possible, and if his heart stopped beating before the ambulance arrived she would have to try to resuscitate.

'What's the problem?' a cool authoritative voice asked from somewhere above her head, and Zoey looked up to see the man from across the road observing her.

'Suspected heart attack,' she said briefly.

He quickly knelt beside her and observed the removal man.

'I'm ready to resuscitate if he stops breathing,' she told him, 'but at the moment he's just about holding on.'

'I'll take over,' he said in that same cool voice. 'In this sort of situation amateurs can do more harm than good. So if you'll just give me some space…'

'I know exactly what I'm doing,' she told him, equally coolly. 'In any case, the ambulance will be here any second.' And because she was totally frazzled with one thing on top of another, she added, 'They'll be treating it as a red alert.'

That would show him that she knew what she was about!

'A-agh!' the man cried as the pain attacked him again, and Zoey thought contritely that this poor fellow wouldn't care who looked after him as long as somebody did.

Within the next few seconds the ambulance came screeching into the quiet cul-de-sac and Zoey and the stranger moved to one side to let the paramedics take over.

As it speeded off into the chilly autumn night, Zoey breathed a sigh of relief. The coronary unit was where he needed to be. There was little that she could have done for him in the circumstances, except to be there, ready to act if the worst had happened.

The lad, who'd been agog while it had all been happening, was now facing up to his predicament as he said, 'I can't carry this stuff in on me own.'

'No, of course not,' she agreed. 'I'll help you. We'll manage somehow.'

'I take it that you're in the process of moving in,' the stranger said.

'Er…yes. I am,' she said awkwardly.

Why didn't he go away? She had enough to cope with at the moment without having to make polite conversation with this rather patronising man.

His glance was on Mandy and Rosie.

'If you'd both like to go inside before the baby gets cold, I'll help this young fellow to bring in your stuff.'

Zoey wanted to tell him that they would manage, but she was tired, and devastated at what had just happened to the removal man.

So she nodded meekly and said, 'Thanks for the offer…and then I'll have to see about getting the lad home and the van back to where it belongs.'

'One thing at a time,' he said calmly, and again she was irritated by his manner. It was almost as if he thought that here was some female who wasn't coping very well and he'd better sort her out.

In a short space of time her bed, dressing-table and wardrobe had been placed in a bedroom at the front of the house, her clothes had been brought in ready to be hung up and her computer placed in the room that her father had used as an office.

Then the man told her, 'I'm going to take the lad home and will call to see the sick man's family on the way to tell them what's happened…if that's all right with you.'

Instead of being appropriately grateful, she muttered, 'Yes, of course,' and thought that maybe he'd like to tell her what time to go to bed and what time to get up in the morning, too.

He smiled for the first time.

'Nothing in this life is ever as simple as we would like it to be, is it?' And off he went, taking the spike-haired youth across the road to where his car was parked.

'Thank goodness for that,' she breathed when they'd gone. Turning to Mandy, she gave a tired smile. 'What a catastrophe! Maybe now we can settle down.' As her young stepmother led the way into the house, Zoey asked her how her day had been.

Mandy shrugged her thin shoulders.

'The same as always…awful.'

Zoey groaned inwardly. It was hard to cope with Mandy's constant depression. She was grieving herself. But most of the time she had to contain it while she cheered up the young widow.

They'd had a meal of sorts and Zoey had taken over Rosie's bathtime so that Mandy could have an early night. Now, much as she would have liked to have been able to fall into bed herself, she felt that she couldn't do that until the man who'd helped them came back.

She'd been churlish and snappy with him and felt that she should make amends, if only by thanking him properly. The fact that he'd seemed out to rub her up the wrong way would have to be ignored.

At last she saw his car draw up outside the house opposite and, not wanting to accost him on the road, she waited until he'd gone inside.

When he opened the door to her ring on the bell she was able to take stock of him properly for the first time, and she caught her breath as unreadable dark eyes above a firm jawline met hers.

The hair matched the eyes. Almost black…in a stylish cut that accentuated the strong stem of his neck and lay smoothly above his brow.

Wow! she thought. I must have been really wound up earlier not to have registered this guy!

But she'd been too engrossed in being irritated by him to have taken note of his physical attractions.

'Ah! It's you,' he said. 'I was going to make my report in the morning as it's late.'

It seemed that he wasn't going to ask her in so Zoey prepared to say her piece on the doorstep.

'I know that, but I had to come across to thank you properly for helping out. I was so stressed earlier I must have seemed inappreciative and I'm sorry.'

He smiled…again.

'No problem. I saw the lad safely home and then went to see the patient's family. Needless to say, they were very upset and I've been wondering since if there was any news of him.'

Zoey nodded.

'Yes. I phoned a short time ago. He's in Coronary Care and responding to treatment. That was all they would tell me.'

'Good,' he said dismissively. 'So maybe we can both now relax and you can forget your somewhat hectic arrival at the house across the way.'

She sighed.

'Yes. I've come to live with my stepmother. She's all alone with little Rosie and needs my help. So I've transferred from the main fire station in the city and moved to the local one here in this country backwater. Where no doubt I'll find Pugh, Pugh, or Barney Magrew maybe.'

He pursed his lips and she realised that he wasn't amused.

'I doubt it,' he said blandly, and then to make her feel even more guilty he looked pointedly at his watch and said, 'If you'll excuse me, I'm about to prepare my belated evening meal.'

'Of course,' she mumbled apologetically. Turning away, she hurried back to her new lodgings.

When he'd closed the door Alex Carradine leant against it and let out a deep breath. So the girl with eyes like sapphires in a pert face framed by a golden bob was Zoey Lawrence, the trauma technician about to join the team at the fire station tomorrow. What a turn-up for the book!

That was his first thought. The second was that it was fortunate that most of the guys there were happily married. With the exception of himself and Leading Fireman Greg Osbourne, who was away on a course.

That one would create havoc if she started swaying those trim hips around the place and flashing those incredible eyes. Having a woman on the staff wasn't unusual. It had happened once or twice before, but they'd been of a more staid appearance than Zoey Lawrence.

Her tight black trousers, skimpy white top and shoes that lifted her a good three inches off the ground were fashionable to say the least. But thankfully tomorrow she would be dressed more soberly in the dark blue uniform of the fire services.

It was a pity they'd started off on the wrong foot. It had been one of those days. Lots of red tape to deal with from headquarters in the absence of the station officer who'd suddenly taken early retirement.

Then a call to a false alarm, followed by a distressing house fire in the late afternoon. And as if that hadn't been enough, Gloria had come through on his mobile to say that she would be in the area in the near future and could he put her up for a few days?

He'd said it would be no problem, but had wished that she would stay away now that they were divorced. It had been strange, the way their marriage had foundered. They'd been friends for a long time before they'd decided to marry...even as far back as junior school, which everyone had thought would make their union as solid as a rock.

But maybe they'd known each other too well as it hadn't worked. They'd got on each other's nerves soon after the event, realising that their friendship had endured because there had been no ties to it and that marriage could be an irksome thing.

The break, when it had come, had been amicable enough and now they were going their separate ways with no acrimony on either side. Alex was thankful they'd had no children. He would have stuck it out if they had.

All in all it had been a chastening experience and he had decided that it would be a long time before he made another commitment...if ever.

When he'd seen what had been happening over the road he'd gone across to see what the problem was, and it had gone on from there with the blonde girl and himself becoming reluctant acquaintances.

Gloria and he had moved into the house in the cul-de-sac when they'd got married and he had bought her half from her when they'd divorced, opting to stay there because it was close to the fire station.

It was a requirement of all personnel that they live within a short distance of the place, so as to be able to respond quickly to any emergency when not on site.

Vaguely aware that a young widow with a baby lived opposite, he hadn't taken much notice…until today. And now he had a feeling that, whether he wanted to or not, he was going to get to know the folk in the house opposite a lot better.

While eating his solitary meal, Alex found himself smiling. That young madam with her Pugh, Pugh, Barney Magrew. Did she think they were all yokels in the countryside? It looked as if tomorrow might turn out to be a very interesting day.

As Zoey walked the short distance to the fire station the next morning it seemed strange not to have high-rise buildings around her and the deafening noise of city traffic in her ears.

She could hear birds chirping in the trees and the air smelt fresh and clean. Her step lightened. She had done the right thing, coming here. Mandy seemed brighter already now that she wasn't so alone.

Zoey had given Rosie her early morning bottle and had then tucked her up with her mother, having made Mandy promise that she wouldn't mope all day, and now it was time to get into the swing of things in her new surroundings.

After only a short time amongst her new colleagues she had to admit that she'd been too quick to prejudge them. They were friendly and obviously efficient and well trained if their conversation was anything to go by.

If there were a few warm glances coming her way she chose to ignore them.

The only civilian employee on the station was the cleaner, Dorothea, a plump, motherly being who eyed Zoey's slenderness and commented laughingly that she could do with some flesh on her bones. A suggestion that was immediately vetoed by the crew.

'The station officer has just taken early retirement on the grounds of ill health,' one of them told her. 'He was due to go soon anyway, and we're expecting that Sub-officer Alex Carradine will eventually take over. He's been to a meeting at headquarters this morning, and has just phoned to say that he'll be back any moment.'

As if on cue, the door was opening and as Zoey turned round her jaw went slack.

'Good morning,' the man from the house across the road said. 'If you'd like to step into the office, Zoey, I think we need to have a chat.'

She swallowed hard.

'Yes, of course,' she croaked. Following him meekly, she lowered herself onto a grey plastic chair opposite a big wooden desk.

When he'd seated himself facing her, Alex said smoothly, 'Sorry to disappoint you, but the name is Carradine. Alex Carradine. Not Cuthbert, Dibble or Grubb.'

Zoey bent her head as her cheeks began to burn.

'I'm sorry. I didn't know who I was talking to when I said that.'

'Obviously. How could you?' he murmured.

'Why didn't you tell me who you were when I explained that I was coming to work here?'

'Why should I? It seemed a pity to knock sideways all your preconceived ideas.' His eyes were on the paperwork that he'd just deposited on the desk. 'But shall we get down to business?'

Zoey nodded mutely.

'I had wondered why you were seeking a transfer from the main fire station. What you told me last night gave me the answer,' he said with the smooth tone crisping up. 'I've received details of the training you've received in first aid and at the accident and emergency department of the city's main hospital, and your function here will be the same as before, but on a smaller scale.

'As you will be aware, most stations have a trauma technician on the team to give emergency medical assistance when needed. Either before the ambulance arrives, in conjunction with paramedics, or even instead of them if their help isn't required.

'There's a good atmosphere at this station. We are all friends who meet socially as well as being workmates. There are no disruptive influences and I want it to stay that way.

'I'm aware that you are used to working in a more sophisticated setting than this and you won't find the same sort of night-life here as you would find in the city. You may have to look further afield.'

Zoey eyed him mutinously. What did he think she was? Some pleasure loving sex-pot? Her social life had been non-existent for months while she'd been doing a very demanding job and spending every spare minute with Mandy and the baby. And in any case, what had it got to do with Alex Carradine what she did in her free time?

But not being prepared to let him discover that her evenings were far from pleasure-filled, she said easily, 'I'll find the nightspots when I need them, never fear.'

'Hmm. I'm sure you will,' he agreed unsmilingly. 'I

take it that you've met all the firemen based here with the exception of Leading Fireman Osbourne.'

'Yes, I have,' she told him, now in subdued tones.

Everything had been fine until this man had appeared to dampen her spirits. What did he have against her? He hadn't even seen her in action. But he had, hadn't he, after a fashion? And he'd wanted to know if she knew what she was doing. Well, she would show him just that. That she definitely did know what she was doing.

'We have just the one engine at this station,' he was saying, 'and when a "shout" comes we all go out on it, with myself in charge. Is that clear?'

'Perfectly.'

'Good. As Bonfire Night will soon be here, we will be going to the schools over the next couple of weeks to lecture the pupils about the dangers of fireworks, and a week on Saturday we are doing a charity "pull" for the local hospital's children's ward.'

His glance went to her slim shoulders.

'You may want to think about that before committing yourself. A fire-engine is some weight to pull and the straps over our shoulders can bite a bit.'

Zoey shook her fair mop, brushing away dismal thoughts of what working alongside teaching staff sometimes led to.

'I'd like to take part if you don't mind. It sounds like fun and it's for a good cause.'

'Fine. Just as you wish. You know where to go for a dislocated shoulder, I take it?'

She didn't answer, just glared at him, and he said dismissively, 'I think that's all for now, Zoey. If you have any kind of problems, come to me. I repeat...any kind. Right?'

She nodded obediently, while vowing not to if she could help it.

'Maybe you wouldn't mind asking those guys out there if there's any tea and toast left from the elevenses,' he said, and picked up the top sheet off the papers on the desk.

When she'd gone, Alex leaned back in his chair and gazed pensively through the window. He was treating this bright young woman as if he was dubious about her joining the team. What was the matter with him?

She hadn't put a foot wrong so far, except by being quite stunning. Had his marriage flop really made his attitude towards young attractive women so negative?

The information he'd received about Zoey Lawrence said that she was twenty-four. He wasn't that much older than her, eight years or so, and yet he was laying down the law like some crabby Methuselah. The first opportunity that came along he would show her that he was human...and fair.

Engine and crew were called out at midday. Three youths in a car had crashed on a narrow bend on one of the local hill roads and the police had asked for their assistance in freeing one of them who was still trapped in the car.

Within minutes they were off, wearing their fireproof jackets and yellow helmets, with Zoey displaying a green and white flash on hers to denote she was the trauma technician.

Geoff Baines, an affable, middle-aged father of two, was in the driving seat with Alex beside him. The rest of them were in the back.

Alex turned round and his eyes met hers, yet what he had to say was for all of them, or so she thought.

'Remember,' he warned them, 'don't release the victim too fast without medical help on hand or...what? You tell us, Zoey,' he said in a milder tone than he'd used before.

'Sure,' she said easily. 'The "crush syndrome" can occur. The extensive damage to the muscles causes protein pigments to be released into the bloodstream, causing temporary kidney failure. That causes substances usually excreted in the urine to build up to toxic levels in the blood. Without prompt dialysis the kidney failure will be fatal.'

As the men clapped at the end of her description of the perils awaiting someone who had been severely crushed, Zoey gave a saucy little bow and, watching her, Alex had to smile. Whatever she did, Zoey was certainly going to brighten up the place.

Of the three youths in the car when it had gone out of control on the hill bend, one was standing in a daze, too shocked to comprehend properly what had happened. Another was unconscious by the roadside, with paramedics attending him, and the third was trapped in the car which had overturned when it had hit the stone wall by the roadside.

He was crushed beneath the twisted metal of the seats and the sun-roof, and it was immediately obvious to the fire crew why they'd been called to assist.

His arm was hanging limply through the window and while Zoey ran across to apply pressure on the forearm in an attempt to contain heavy bleeding, Alex and Geoff got out the Combi tools and connected them to the petrol-powered generator that would provide the hydraulic pressure needed for their steel jaws to cut away the framework of the car.

Both men had put on goggles with visors attached to

protect their faces from flying fragments as they worked, and another of the team was holding a teardrop-shaped plastic shield to protect the casualty from a similar hazard.

'Cutting!' the cry went up, to warn anyone close by to stand back. With Alex at the front of the car, beginning to slice through what the men called the 'A' post, which in ordinary jargon was the metal that held the windscreen, and Geoff doing his bit at the 'C' post, the framework at the back of the window area, they began to clear the way to the injured youth.

The noise of the generator and the cutting equipment was deafening, blotting out all other sounds, and when Zoey looked up she saw that the 'smart' team from Accident and Emergency had arrived.

Two doctors and two nurses were spilling out onto the road beside them, which made the turn-out of the emergency services complete. Police, ambulance, fire service and the staff from A and E, who were called out when surgery on the spot might be required, such as amputations.

Amazingly the lad was still alive and as the last piece of metal was cut away there was a sigh of relief from all those present.

He'd been given an injection for pain and as they slowly eased him out onto a spinal board he was drifting in and out of consciousness.

As the fire team prepared to leave the scene, the senior policeman in charge came over.

'Well done, lads,' he said.

Zoey smiled. In the bulky coat and with the helmet on her head she looked no different from the rest. Alex Carradine would be pleased about that.

* * *

Later in the day Alex rang to see how the three victims of the car crash were, and as the rest of them waited anxiously for the report Zoey was amazed how she'd settled in so quickly. It was as if she'd never worked anywhere else.

'One lad treated for shock and then discharged,' Alex informed them as he put the phone down. 'The guy who was lying in the road has severe concussion and a fractured arm and leg. And our young friend who came off worst is in Intensive Care with multiple injuries...but they seem to think he'll live. I suggest that some of us call in to see him when he's stabilised. What do you think?'

'Yes, sure thing,' Geoff said, and the rest nodded their agreement.

When Alex saw Zoey's surprised expression he said, 'Sometimes we get a case like today's and it gets to us more than others. Maybe it was the look of silent pleading in the kid's eyes as we tried to free him. Or because they were just reckless youngsters who might have had their lives cut short. I don't know.

'The lad who was trapped lives near one of our guys, which makes it all the more personal. So we'll follow it up. It stands to reason that in an area like this we're much more likely to find it's someone we know when we get a call-out than in one of the bigger stations.'

'Yes, I suppose so,' Zoey said, adding with unconscious wistfulness, 'Though it's not likely to happen to me as I don't know anybody.'

'We'll soon put that right,' one of the men said. 'Meet us in the pub tonight, Zoey. We'll introduce you to our wives.'

Her smile was wry.

'I can't. I'm here to give my young stepmother support and she won't want me to leave her the moment I've arrived.'

'Bring her with you.'

She was conscious of dark, inscrutable eyes watching her as she told them, 'It's not that easy. She has a young baby.'

Remembering Alex Carradine's comments earlier in the day when he'd called her into the office, she thought that he would have expected her to jump at the chance of mixing with the locals as the next best thing to flaunting herself beneath city lights.

When she arrived back at Mandy's place Zoey's face brightened. Mandy had cleaned up the house and in the afternoon had taken Rosie to the baby clinic in the nearby community centre.

Both activities were a step in the right direction as the house had badly needed freshening up and previously Mandy hadn't even bothered to have Rosie weighed.

Zoey gave her a hug.

'Well done, Mandy,' she encouraged her. 'The place looks like a palace. What sort of a report did you get on Rosie?'

'It was all right,' she said with slightly more zest than usual. 'They said she was healthy and putting on weight nicely, but that I must see she gets plenty of fresh air as she's rather pale.'

'Good. The fresh air should be no problem. All it needs is for you to get out a bit more.'

'About getting out more,' Mandy said. 'Some of the mothers from the clinic are going out for a pizza tonight and they asked me to join them. What do you think?'

What did she think?

'I think you should go,' Zoey told her firmly. 'You've

been shut away in this place long enough. I'll see to Rosie.'

Mandy's face lit up and Zoey thought, I don't believe I'm seeing this. Was there a light at the end of the tunnel at last? If Mandy was going to come out of the depression that had swamped her ever since her husband's death, putting her own life on hold would have been well worthwhile, she decided.

When Mandy had gone, looking almost like her old self, and Rosie had been tucked up for the night, Zoey stood looking at the house opposite.

What would Alex be doing at this moment? she wondered. Off to the pub to join the others? Or spending the evening with his family? There'd been no mention of him having a wife but it stood to sense that there would be someone. He was far too attractive to be unattached.

She was tidying up the kitchen after the evening meal when the doorbell rang. When she opened the door he was there. Almost as if she'd willed him to appear.

'Alex!' she said in a voice that wasn't quite steady. 'What brings you here?'

He didn't reply for a moment. If he were to answer truthfully he would have to say that he wasn't sure, and that wouldn't sound much like a man of purpose.

She was stepping back.

'Come in, but, please, don't make a noise as I've just got Rosie to sleep. That little one doesn't know the meaning of slumber.'

He smiled as he stepped over the threshold and this time it was a proper one, not just a relaxing of the face muscles.

'Where's her mother?' he asked in a low voice.

Zoey couldn't resist it.

'Gone gallivanting. I'm baby-minding.'

'So that's why you turned down the invitation to go to the pub.'

She shook her blonde bob.

'No, not exactly. I didn't know what I'd be doing until I got home as Mandy is a bit unpredictable these days. She hasn't got over my father's death. They hadn't been married long.'

'You've lost your father, then,' he said with swift concern. 'I'm sorry to hear that. And what about your grief? Who's helping you through it?'

Zoey stared at him. She could feel tears pricking. He was the first person who'd realised that Mandy wasn't the only one who'd been bereaved.

Then to her horror the tears were spilling down her cheeks. She turned away as the torrent of misery unleashed itself, horrified that this should happen in front of Alex of all people, only to find herself pulled gently round again into a pair of sheltering arms.

'Let it out,' he said quietly. 'Is this the first time you've wept?'

'Yes,' she gulped.

'Then it's overdue. Bottling up emotions never did anyone any good, Zoey. I should know.'

Her sobs were subsiding but she didn't move out of his arms.

'There was never time to grieve,' she choked. 'Mandy and the baby needed me so much.'

He tilted her chin with a gentle finger and as she looked up at him with reddened eyes he told her, 'I only came across to ask if you'd enjoyed your first day.'

She managed a smile.

'Yes. It was great.'

'All of it?'

'Well, apart from the lecture I received at one point.'

'Standard procedure,' he said blandly, but knew it not to be true. He'd acted like he had because he had a gut feeling that the newest member of staff at the small fire station was going to be a disturbing influence.

Zoey was wiping her eyes and moving out of his arms, and Alex knew he didn't want her to do that. She'd felt frail, vulnerable, and her perfume was as light and tantalising as Zoey herself. He couldn't remember when last he'd held a woman as close as this. But he knew she was doing the right thing, or he would be falling into his own trap.

'Thanks for being there for me in a dark moment, Alex,' she croaked. 'I had no intention of burdening you with my problems.'

'I did tell you to come to me if you had any, didn't I?' he told her, not knowing quite what to say. 'Though I didn't think it would be so soon.'

Was that meant to tell her she was being a nuisance? she wondered. That she'd no sooner arrived on the scene than she was demanding his attention?

'Yes, well, it won't happen again,' she told him.

As he began to try to explain what he'd really meant they heard the baby crying up above.

'I'll see you tomorrow,' he said, and as Zoey pointed herself towards the stairs he went.

CHAPTER TWO

As ZOEY soothed Rosie back to sleep again her thoughts were chaotic. She'd really let her grief show for the first time since losing her dad, and whose arms had she ended up in? Those of a tall dark stranger. And what was more, she'd been enough aware of him to enjoy it, in spite of her tears.

It was incredible that he of all people had realised how little time she'd had to come to terms with her own hurt. She hardly knew Alex, was wary of his brusque approach, and yet for an amazing few seconds she'd felt cherished—and that wasn't a feeling she experienced very often.

'Your big sister's going all soppy, and it won't do,' she told the now slumbering Rosie. 'Not with that man anyway. He's not sure what to make of me, but "bimbo" is a word that springs to mind.'

After tonight's incident she wouldn't know how to look him in the face in the morning. Her face softened. Yet he had been kind. And what had he hinted about bottling up one's feelings…that if anybody knew about that, he did?

Maybe she might ask a few questions about him in the morning. Just to get a picture of what made him tick…or otherwise. Merely out of curiosity, of course.

From what she'd seen of him so far, Alex wasn't likely to be attracted to anyone like herself, and for her part she could think of lots of men more appealing than him…couldn't she? In any case, she wasn't looking for romance. She'd recently had her fill of male ego.

Mandy came home from her night out with the young mothers almost animated. Her cheeks were flushed, eyes bright, and Zoey thought, This is what she's short of. Her stepmother was only a few years older than herself. Her father wouldn't have wanted her to waste her young life grieving for him.

'So I take it you enjoyed yourself,' she said, as they sat by the fire with mugs of hot chocolate before going to bed.

'Yes, I did,' Mandy admitted. With heightened colour, she went on, 'I knocked my drink over and the man who owned the place was really nice about it. He came and mopped it up and brought me another one. I felt such a fool, and told him it was a long time since I'd been out socialising. He asked me why and when I told him he was really sorry.'

Zoey's eyes were dancing.

'Not bad for your first foray back into the wicked world.'

Mandy smiled.

'It didn't feel wicked to me. It felt lovely.'

'Mmm,' Zoey agreed. 'It's been a nice night all round.'

'But you haven't been anywhere.'

'True,' Zoey agreed, 'but with a beautiful baby to care for and a neighbourly visit from a most intriguing man, what more could I ask for?'

'You don't mean the good Samaritan from last night?'

'Yes. I do.'

'And?'

'And…nothing. He merely called to see if I'd enjoyed my first day.'

What Mandy would say if she heard the rest was something Zoey wasn't going to risk at that moment, and with a yawn she said, 'I'm off to bed. Sweet dreams of your pizza man.'

Zoey tried not to smile as the young widow went bright red, but her step was lighter as she climbed the stairs. They were an all-female household. Some male blood was needed to level the scales. Whose, though?

The next morning Alex Carradine greeted her as if they hadn't had any contact since leaving the station the night before, and Zoey got the message. He'd obviously decided that if the job brought them together that was fine. But he was going to treat what had happened when he'd called round to see her as a one-off, triggered by circumstances.

All right, she thought rebelliously. What did he think she was going to do? Make something out of a special moment they'd shared?

It was quiet during the morning with little to occupy the staff, but in the early afternoon it all changed. A public house not far away, which had been boarded up prior to demolition at some future date, was on fire.

When they got there it was clear that unless the blaze was brought under control quickly it would spread to neighbouring shops and houses.

'There are no services at this place,' Alex informed them, 'so it looks as if it might be arson. Either kids messing about, or a grudge against the brewery maybe. Whatever it is, let's get it under control.'

At that moment a woman who had just arrived on the scene told them, 'There's been a tramp sleeping in there for the last week.'

'Right,' Alex said decisively as they uncoupled the

hoses, 'it seems that we might have a ''persons reported'' on our hands. Zoey, get back to Control and tell them what's happening. The rest of you look out for a person somewhere in the building. He might be long gone but we can't take any chances.'

While she was making the call, Alex and two of the team disappeared into the smoke-filled public house wearing breathing apparatus while the others tackled the blaze from the outside. Zoey was about to follow them into the building when it became apparent that the woman's warning had been timely. The tramp had been inside and now he was being carried to safety by the firemen.

They laid him on the ground some distance away from the blaze and Alex said, 'He's barely conscious, Zoey. Get the oxygen to him while I radio for an ambulance.'

As she put the mask over the man's face, she could smell alcohol. That was the last thing he'd needed around him in a burning building. It was a wonder he hadn't gone up in flames, but the fates had been kind and as he began to breathe more easily she thought grimly that but for a comment from a bystander this fellow wouldn't have survived.

Fortunately he had no burns. His main problem was smoke inhalation, and once his breathing had stabilised the tramp would have some questions to answer.

Alex was back and nodding his satisfaction to see the man responding to treatment. Then he turned and said briefly, 'We're going back in there to make sure there was no one else with him. Stay with him until the ambulance arrives, Zoey.'

She didn't need telling. It was her job to give medical assistance. They all had to do it at times, but hers was the role of trauma technician. Yet she did wonder if Alex was keeping her in the background because she was a woman.

It was to be hoped that wasn't the case. She wouldn't be doing the job if she wanted to be treated differently from the men. Whatever she looked like on the outside, she was just as capable as the rest of them. Not as strong maybe, but there were ways to overcome that sort of handicap. Quick thinking and agility always came in handy.

At last the fire was under control. The vagrant had been taken to hospital for observation and it now remained for the fire crew to return to base and the local authority to make a decision on how soon the demolition could begin.

Alex had been right when he'd said there was no gas or electricity supply to the premises. But they hadn't reckoned with an intruder making a fire from rubbish he'd found lying around and then dropping off into a drunken sleep.

Zoey had a feeling that the fire crew wouldn't be following this one up, but she was wrong.

'That fellow needs some proper accommodation when he's discharged from hospital,' Alex said when they got back, 'and if the health authority doesn't do anything about it, I will.'

They hadn't been back at base long when the phone in the rest room rang, and as she was nearest to it Zoey picked it up.

'Put Alex on the line, will you?' an authoritative voice said in her ear.

'Who shall I tell him is calling?' she asked.

The question was answered by another.

'Are you new, or something?'

'Yes,' she answered coolly, suddenly on the defensive.

'And so who are you, then?'

'My name's Zoey Lawrence. I've just been transferred here,' she said levelly. 'And you are?'

'Er, just tell him that Gloria's on the line.'

Alex had come out of the office and was observing her questioningly.

'Someone called Gloria for you,' she told him as she handed him the phone.

'Thanks,' he said briefly, and waited until she'd moved out of earshot before answering.

'Who's Gloria?' she asked of Geoff when Alex went back into the other room. 'And why didn't she ring him on the office phone?'

'Gloria is his ex-wife and she came though on this extension because he's usually in here with us,' he explained. 'Was she coming the queen bee with you?'

'A bit.'

'That's Gloria. She's not a bad sort but inclined to be a bit pushy where Alex is concerned. Normally he would be no pushover in anybody's book, but he always has time for that one.'

'Yet you say they're divorced?'

'Yes. It was an amicable affair. No other persons involved. Not as far as he was concerned anyway.'

'No children, then?'

'No. For which he's truly thankful.'

'You mean that he didn't want any?'

'No. Certainly not that. More because he wouldn't have wanted them to get hurt by a marriage break-up.'

'I see,' she said thoughtfully.

Some of the questions she'd intended asking had been

answered, and now she was curious about the woman who'd taken his name and slept in his bed…and was still in touch.

They were due at the local comprehensive school the next day to talk about fire safety in the forthcoming bonfire season. As they left the station the team was in relaxed mood. On this occasion there would be no hazards awaiting them at the other end. Unless facing a hall full of teenage pupils could be termed as one.

When the youngsters crowded round after the lecture had finished, Zoey found that as usual her presence was creating some interest. With the boys because her youthful glamour was unexpected in such an occupation, and from some of the girls who expressed a desire to join the fire service themselves after meeting her, though whether it was to help the community or to be in the company of a group of macho men, she wasn't sure. Which brought back to mind painful memories of Damien's dallyings with a teacher from one of the schools they'd visited.

Her own decision to become part of the vital emergency service stemmed from when she was twelve years old and a young plumber working at her parent's house had left his wife and child safely at home, only to be told an hour later that she'd tried to light a coal fire with paraffin and had set the place on fire.

Members of the fire service had risked their lives to get the woman and child out of the blazing house, and Zoey had never forgotten their bravery or the young husband's gratitude. She'd known then it was what she wanted to do and had never swerved from her purpose.

The physical fitness tests she'd had to pass had been gruelling, but she'd come through them and soon after being accepted had decided that she wanted to be a trauma technician.

And now here she was. Out of her environment and surprisingly not regretting it. For one thing, Mandy had bucked up almost from the moment of her arrival, and for another…there was Alex Carradine. Everyone had a good word for him except herself.

Yet that wasn't strictly true, was it? She'd acknowledged his kindness when she'd wept in his arms. Admitted that he was extremely high up in the presentable male stakes. But she wasn't too keen on the way he seemed to be dubious about her.

For one thing, he seemed to think that because she was young and liked to be fashionable, she was trouble. He expected her to be pleasure-loving and materialistically minded. If he only knew. It had been months since she'd been anywhere other than work or Mandy's.

The ex-wife sounded as if she was still in the picture. Maybe it wasn't surprising that Alex was a bit edgy. On the other hand, if there'd been no hard feelings maybe he was happy to still have her around.

Every time Alex thought about the break-up of his marriage there was relief in him that it was over. It had been a monumental mistake and he was still plagued by it.

The weird thing was that he and Gloria had always got on so well until they'd lived under the same roof, and then it had all fallen apart.

He'd found that in some ways they'd known each other too well and in others hadn't known each other at all. The marriage had lacked the mystery and magic that made each day something to look forward to and the predictability of life with Gloria had made him realise that he'd made a big mistake.

It would have been awful if they'd been his sentiments only, but she'd felt the same and so the break, when it had come, had been a lot less painful than it might have been. Though he did sometimes feel that she was finding it harder to adjust than he was.

His main problem was regret that they hadn't stayed just friends and looked elsewhere for marriage partners. Because now they'd ended up not anything at all, except maybe polite acquaintances.

Gloria had been a solicitor with a local practice and he'd sometimes wondered if her unimaginative legal approach to the job had spilled over too much into their lives.

She'd moved to the London area after the divorce, taking up a position with a firm of solicitors there, and seemed happy enough with the arrangement. She phoned from time to time, and on the day that Zoey had answered her call had said, 'So you've got a new woman working with you now?'

'Yes.'

'What's she like?'

As he'd glanced through the office window to where Zoey had been chatting to Geoff, with the rays of an autumn sun turning her blonde bob to silver, he'd felt that for some reason he didn't want to discuss Zoey Lawrence with his ex-wife.

So he'd merely said, 'Seems all right, but it's early days yet.' Veering away from any further discussion about her, he'd asked smoothly, 'What can I do for you, Gloria?'

It had been then that she'd asked if she could stay with him for a while and with no real reason to refuse he'd agreed.

*   *   *

In the days that followed Zoey continued to adjust to a more rural lifestyle. In her free time she pushed Rosie in her pram along country lanes and beside the canal that wound its way between woodland and green meadows, enjoying the feeling of space and breathing in the fresh untainted air.

She sometimes thought that Alex Carradine would be surprised if he knew how much pleasure it gave her, being in this place, as for some reason he'd got her labelled as a typical townie.

Her forays into the countryside with the baby gave Mandy the chance to have some time to herself, and their domestic situation was improving all the time.

On a Sunday afternoon she spotted Alex coming towards her with a frisky red setter on the lead. As they drew level Zoey found herself suddenly tongue-tied. It was the first time they'd met outside working hours since the night she'd wept in his arms and she wondered if it was as clear in his memory as it was in hers.

'Hello, there,' he said, and as she stooped to fondle the dog he bent over the pram. 'Beautiful baby. What's her name?'

'Rosie,' she said awkwardly.

'Hmm, nice. I take it that you're very fond of her?'

'I adore her.'

'Yes, but shouldn't you be doing your own thing occasionally instead of constantly being child-minder? You're certainly full of surprises.'

'I'm not sure how to take that comment, but I have a feeling that there is criticism in it somewhere. Are you saying that I'm not living up to your expectations of what a city girl wants?' she said, with a breezy sort of nonchalance now that the first strained moments of meeting had passed.

'Now, why would you think that?' he asked with a smile.

'Because I don't fit into the mould perhaps?'

Alex was serious now.

'There is no mould. We are all what we are, Zoey. Life would be just too boring if we were all the same.'

She waited for him to go on but he was changing the subject.

'How far are you going?' he asked, as the dog pulled at the lead.

'Just to the end of the lane and then I'm turning back,' she told him.

'We'll walk with you, then. Gipsy has had enough exercise for one day.'

'Why Gipsy?'

'Because when I first got him he was roving all over the place, straining to be free.'

'So why not Rover?'

'Too mundane for a livewire such as this dog.'

Their respective dwellings were in sight and when they stopped outside Mandy's house Zoey was loath to end their brief time together.

'Until tomorrow, then,' Alex said, and for a moment she let herself imagine that he was as reluctant to go his own way as she was.

'Yes,' she agreed, 'and regarding your earlier remark that I'm full of surprises, watch this space.'

As dark brows rose questioningly she laughed and, wheeling the pram up the path, left him to ponder.

The men from the station had repeated their invitation to join them one evening in the pub and the next night Zoey took them at their word and turned up at the old inn that was a popular place of refreshment for ramblers, motorists and the local folk.

It had been a stressful day at the fire station. They'd attended a house fire and had brought a young child out just in the nick of time. They'd also been called to a head-on car crash where an elderly man had suffered a heart attack at the wheel and as he'd lost control had swerved into the path of a vehicle going in the opposite direction.

The casualties had been trapped and the fire service had been called out to separate the two cars with a Tifor winch...a steel cable passing through a winding mechanism and operated by a lever.

The elderly motorist had been pronounced dead at the scene, but the woman driver of the other car had miraculously survived, with Zoey putting a temporary splint on a broken leg and administering pain relief until the arrival of the ambulance.

And now, for some light relief, she'd come to The Wheatsheaf Inn.

She was introduced to wives and girlfriends and might have felt out of it if there hadn't been someone else there on his own.

Alex appeared halfway through the evening and after observing her with the same surprised expression as when they'd separated the day before he came across to say, 'So you've taken note of what I said yesterday.'

She smiled, turning the full brilliance of her sapphire gaze upon him.

'Yes, I've been let out for the evening.'

'Good for you. Let me buy you a drink.'

'How about introducing me first?' a voice said from behind her, and as she swung round Zoey found herself looking into a strange face.

'Ah, yes,' Alex said levelly. 'Zoey, this is Greg Osbourne. The only member of the team you haven't already met. Greg's been away on a course.'

'I'd have been back earlier if I'd known what I was missing,' the newcomer remarked smoothly as light hazel eyes looked Zoey over.

He was of medium height with brown hair and a trim physique, and seemed pleasant enough. She might even have given him a second glance if Alex hadn't been around, but he was, and the more she saw of him, the more Zoey liked what she saw.

But she hadn't forgotten Damien. She'd often heard it said that it wasn't a good idea to date the people one worked with, and he'd been a prime example. It was claustrophobic, for one thing. No chance to get away from each other.

Ignoring the comment, Alex said, 'This is Zoey's first visit to The Wheatsheaf. She spends most of her free time baby-minding.'

Greg was eyeing her in disappointment.

'So you're married.'

'No!' she protested laughingly. 'The baby belongs to my stepmother. Rosie is my half-sister.'

'Bet she's as gorgeous as you are,' murmured Greg with a wink.

This one has a smooth tongue, Zoey thought, and saw that she wasn't the only one thinking that. Alex's face had tightened and when someone else claimed Greg's attention Alex steered her to a table in the corner.

'He thinks he can charm the birds out of the trees,' he told her as she settled herself opposite him.

'Well,' she told him breezily, 'some men have it and—'

'Some don't?' he finished off for her. 'Which lot do I come into?'

'Oh, you have it all right,' she said airily, as if the subject was of no particular interest, 'but you keep it well under wraps.'

'I see. So that's what you think of me.'

'Partly. Don't forget you were very abrupt with me when I first came to the station. You still are sometimes. But I make allowances for you.'

She was putting out bait and wondering if he would rise to it. He did.

'Why do you feel you have to do that?' he asked slowly.

'Oh, I don't know. Maybe it's because I sense you're miserable. Did it hurt a lot when your marriage broke up?'

'No, it didn't, as a matter of fact. It was a relief. It had been a big mistake almost from the word go, and as we were both of the same mind there seemed no point in carrying on. It would have been a different matter if we'd had children. But as we hadn't it was a clean break. Or at least it was on my part.'

The door of the old inn opened at that moment and he groaned softly.

'Ugh! Here's Gloria now!'

So this was the woman who hadn't been able to make Alex happy, Zoey thought as the new arrival sighted them at their corner table and came across.

Zoey found that she was bracing herself, yet didn't know why. Gloria looked ordinary enough. Of medium height and build, with light brown hair swept back off a face which was expressing some degree of surprise at seeing Alex with her, she wasn't quite as forbidding as Zoey had expected her to be.

A diversion was taking place. Greg had seen her and was stepping in front of her.

'Hi, Gloria,' Zoey heard him say. 'Nice to see you back amongst us. We've missed you.'

Was he being deliberately tactless? Zoey wondered. Winding up the man who was sitting tensely beside her?

'I've missed all of you, too, Gregory,' Gloria said in a husky voice that made Zoey think of throat pastilles.

He was pointing to a nearby vacant table but Gloria wasn't to be sidetracked any longer.

'I'll see you later,' she promised, and carried on to where Zoey and Alex were sitting.

His face had been completely expressionless while she'd been talking to Greg, and it didn't change when she stood over him and said, 'Aren't you going to introduce me to your young friend, Alex?'

'Yes, of course,' he said flatly, and as he made the introductions Zoey's smile beamed out defiantly.

She felt as if she was being patronised and didn't like it.

'Ah, so you're the girl who answered the phone when I rang that time,' Gloria was saying. 'Zoey, isn't it? Settling in, are you?' She sent a slanting glance at Alex.

'Yes, thank you,' Zoey told her politely, and picked up the jacket that she'd draped across the back of the chair when she and Alex had seated themselves. 'I'll leave you to it. Nice to have met you…Gloria.'

If the other woman had been expecting her to address her as Mrs Carradine, she had another think coming, Zoey decided as she went to join the others. And in any case she wasn't, was she?

When she looked across again Alex was frowning as he listened to what his ex-wife was saying, and Zoey wondered why Gloria didn't leave him alone.

He'd said it had been an amicable divorce, so maybe that was why they were still in touch. Yet Zoey could tell that he hadn't been all that pleased to see Gloria.

He came across a few minutes later and when Zoey eyed him enquiringly he said, 'Gloria's gone round to my place. I've given her the keys to let herself in. She's going to be staying for a few days.'

That was all. No explanation of why the woman he'd been married to had suddenly appeared. Maybe he didn't think it warranted one. After all, she herself was only someone that he worked with.

Yet Alex stayed by Zoey's side for the rest of the evening, and when the crowd from the fire station began the short stroll back to their respective homes he was still there beside her.

There was a full moon in the sky, throwing shadows onto the road as they walked along. Feeling strange, as she always did when they were alone, Zoey said, 'I can't believe how quickly I've got used to this place. I never expected to.'

She could have told him that she couldn't believe how quickly she'd got used to him, too. But that might have been asking for trouble. Especially if he wasn't of a similar mind.

'So you've no regrets?' he questioned casually.

'None. For one thing, I see more of Rosie, even though I was never away from her for long before. I have peace of mind where Mandy's concerned.' She took a deep breath and continued rashly, 'And I've met you.'

That stopped him in his tracks.

'What do you mean by that?'

'Exactly what you think I mean.'

They were facing each other and Zoey thought that

they had all the ingredients to make it into a memorable moment. A harvest moon, the quiet peace of the place, and the two of them alone and unobserved with passions rising. At least hers were. She couldn't vouch for his.

Alex reached out and gripped her arms tightly.

'Listen, Zoey,' he said quietly, 'don't start anything you can't finish. I don't play around with other people's emotions and I don't expect them to play around with mine. If you want to flirt around, fine. But don't do it with me. OK?'

She had stiffened in his grip.

'Yes! OK! But tell me…why do you always expect my feelings to be shallow?'

'I don't.'

'Oh, yes, you do. If you don't like me, say so, and I'll take the hint.'

'How long have you known me?' he asked.

'About a week.'

'So how can you possibly feel as you do?'

'I don't know, as I've had cause to be wary of relationships with those I work with.'

'There you are, then,' he said evenly. 'And I've gone through a marriage break-up that was still very stressful even though there was no acrimony, so we have the answer, don't you think?'

Alex was actually smiling and it really ruffled her feathers as he went on to say, 'But the longer you stand there with moonbeams in your eyes, the more I realise that I want to call your bluff.'

'So why don't you?'

'Because for one thing I hope that you're just teasing.' He touched her cheek fleetingly. 'Go home to your family…and I'll go and see what Gloria is up to.' And before she could protest, he was crossing the road and leaving her no choice but to do as he'd suggested.

As Zoey was about to put her key in the lock, the front door of Mandy's house opened and a strange man stood there, looking at her.

'This is Harry. He's just going,' Mandy said, appearing, red-faced, from behind him. 'He owns the pizza parlour down the road. You remember me telling you about him, Zoey?'

As they shook hands she was taking stock of him. He was fortyish, fair-haired and had a kind mouth. Zoey always looked at people's mouths when assessing their character. It had been only seconds ago that she'd been mesmerised by another mouth, wanting it on hers, and she was still limp with the longing it had aroused in her.

When Harry had gone she asked teasingly, 'And so what is going on, Mandy?'

'I met Harry this morning when I took Rosie to the shops,' she explained uncomfortably. 'He recognised me and we chatted for a while. Then went for coffee as his place doesn't open on a Monday.'

'And?' Zoey probed gently.

'I invited him round this evening. Do you think your dad would have minded?'

Zoey kissed Mandy's pale cheek.

'Of course he wouldn't. I've told you so often that this is what he would want you to do…get on with your life. When are you seeing Harry again?'

'Soon maybe. But tell me what sort of an evening you've had.'

'Thought-provoking.'

'Is that it?'

'Yes, for the moment.' And off Zoey went to bed.

CHAPTER THREE

ALEX found Gloria unpacking when he got back and when he saw the amount of luggage she'd brought with her he eyed it in dismay.

She saw his expression and said quickly, 'I've brought extra clothes as I don't know how long I'll be here.'

He was frowning.

'What's going on, Gloria? Why are you here?'

'Aunt Mary is going into hospital tomorrow for a major heart operation and as she's my only relative I've come back to be near her. And as you said you didn't mind, staying here seemed the logical thing to do.'

'I'm sorry to hear about your aunt,' he said, and meant it.

He knew that Gloria was very fond of the old lady, but he thought ruefully that they were supposed to be going their separate ways. Yet what were a couple of weeks in a lifetime?

'Right, then, I'll leave you to finish your unpacking,' he told her, unable to credit that this was happening. Gloria back under his roof...and Zoey, the young enchantress, just across the road.

The following Saturday was the day of the sponsored 'pull' in aid of the local hospital's children's ward. Everyone was eager to take part in such a good cause and Zoey was amongst them.

Twenty-four fire-service personnel from around the area were going to pull the engine from the nearby town to the city seven miles away. It had been taken there the night before to be suitably decorated.

In two teams of twelve, each person would have nylon webbing straps over one shoulder, attached to a centre strap, and, with a fireman in the driving seat to steer the vehicle, they were going to pull it to its destination.

There was a banner across the front of the engine telling the public what the 'pull' was in aid of, and volunteers were collecting loose change in brightly coloured buckets from the jovial crowd that had gathered.

'I got the impression that Alex wasn't keen for me to take part,' she'd previously told Greg, who always seemed to be hovering near, 'but I intend to.'

'Why not?' he'd said carelessly. 'There'll be enough of us to take the weight. We've done it before and no one came to grief. Mind you, we didn't have any women taking part on those occasions. Maybe he has it in mind for you to be on top of the engine dressed in a bikini,' he'd said with a smirk, 'like some of the floats when there's a carnival.'

'It's more the kind of thing he would expect of me,' she'd said wryly, 'but I'd much rather be with the rest of you, doing my bit for the kids.'

It was a cold, clear morning and Alex, who hadn't raised any objections since his comment when the 'pull' had first been mentioned, had offered to give her a lift.

'There's no point in two of us driving to the starting point,' he'd said. 'I imagine you'll enjoy seeing your old haunts again when you get back to the city. Presuming you've not been back there since you moved in with Mandy.'

Here he was again, she'd thought, expecting her to be pining for the bright lights. With the devil in her, she'd said, 'Yes, I might sign on for a couple of hours' lap dancing if we finish early enough. It's one way of balancing the budget.'

'All right,' he'd conceded. 'Point taken. I'll mind my own business.'

Neither of them had referred to those moments beneath the scudding moon a week ago, and as far as she was concerned that was how it was going to stay. She'd made it clear to Alex that she was attracted to him and what had she got? A lecture. Maybe it was just as well that one of them had some sense.

They were off, with the crowds cheering and waving them on their way. The collectors walked alongside them as they pulled, and a van carrying supplies of food, drink and first-aid equipment brought up the rear.

Zoey had positioned herself at the front of the engine as a gesture to women in the fire service everywhere, and as some wag in the crowd cried, 'Heave ho, blondie,' her smile flashed out.

Alex wasn't far away and after he'd asked her a couple of times if she was all right, he gave up.

Greg had other things on his mind, and when they stopped for a rest he said, 'How about us making a day of it, Zoey, once this is over? A meal and a show perhaps, or we could go clubbing.'

She laughed up at him.

'Why? Have you brought a change of clothes? Or are you intending doing the rounds of the clubs and cafés in your uniform? It's going to be a bit sticky after all this effort.'

He tutted irritably.

'Yes, of course I have. They're inside the engine. I thought that you might have done the same.'

'It never occurred to me,' she told him lightly, and

could have explained that even if it had, she wouldn't have accepted the invitation.

She could also have told him that there was only one man she was interested in. That he was only a few feet away and she couldn't get him out of her mind. That he was a different person away from the fire station and she felt confused and off balance.

Her brief relationship with Damien of the roving eye had left her wary of being too trusting of the opposite sex and she'd had no intentions of getting involved again.

But the way she felt about Alex was different. Losing her father and having to give Mandy and Rosie continual support had taken some of the life out of her. She felt she'd grown up a lot, though she was still the same person underneath, bouncy, generous, imaginative, inclined to be a bit reckless, and incredibly romantic.

And now, since she'd met Alex, it was as if the mantle of maturity had fallen even more firmly upon her. Yet she knew he didn't see her like that. He was all the time expecting her to fulfil the role of dizzy blonde, and it was irksome.

She'd been conscious of his dark watchful gaze upon them while Greg had been chatting her up, and she'd thought wistfully that it would have been nice if he'd had a similar idea.

But she sensed that, no matter how often he might say that his marriage was over, he wasn't finished with Gloria yet. Maybe he still cared more than he was prepared to admit. Or hadn't the heart to desert her completely. There was something. His ex-wife's proprietorial manner was proof of that, and he wasn't a man who would be happy to have loose ends in his life.

By midday the sun was shining strongly and they

stopped again for refreshment. A group of small boys
had gathered round the engine and one of them said to
Alex, 'Can we see inside, mister?'

He smiled and lifted each one of them up in turn.

'I want to be a fireman when I grow up,' one of them
said.

'That's good,' Alex replied with suitable gravity, 'but
it can be a dangerous job, you know.' In an aside to
Zoey, who was standing near, he said, 'That's what the
young guy who was trapped in the car on the hill bend
wants to do when he comes out of hospital.'

'What?'

'Join the service.'

'Maybe he feels he owes it to us.'

'Could be, but the poor lad will have to be a lot fitter
than he is now to be accepted.'

While they'd been stationary some of the volunteers
had dropped out and others had replaced them.

'How about you?' Alex asked Zoey.

Zoey had shaken her head. She was beginning to feel
the strain, due to the unseasonably warm weather more
than anything. But she was the only woman in the pull
and as such felt she was flying the flag for the small
contingent of women in the fire service all over the country.

There was a reception committee waiting for them in
the city centre with the local press in attendance, and
when the engine and those who'd pulled it came into
view, cameras began to flash and a cheer went up from
those who had been waiting to welcome them.

It was a light-hearted moment, yet Zoey felt tears
prick as she thought of why they'd done the charity
'pull'. Some of the children from the hospital had been

allowed out to cheer on the firefighters, and the delighted
expressions on their faces made a lump rise in her throat.

As she wiped the tears away with the back of her
hand, an arm was placed around her shoulders and Alex
said, 'They're all such brave kids. I'm glad we can do
something for them.'

She nodded and smiled.

'So am I.'

The speeches were over, the money had been handed in
and the crowds were dispersing. Alex said to his team,
'Let's go. I don't know about you folks, but I'm ready
for a shower and a change of clothes,' and to Zoey, 'The
guys can drop us off where I've parked my car before
they take the engine back to base.'

Zoey nodded her agreement and within minutes they
were leaving the city limits and moving in the direction
of home.

Shortly after they'd transferred to his car, Alex said,
'I need fuel.' As a garage loomed up in front of them
he turned onto the forecourt.

When he'd gone into the shop to pay, Zoey sat mull-
ing over the day's events. The 'pull' had been a huge
success, but what now?

She reckoned that Alex would just drop her off and
that would be that. If she hadn't any plans for the hours
ahead, it didn't mean that he didn't.

He was having to queue, standing head and shoulders
above the rest, and she thought that when he got back
into the car she was going to try to make him see how
he was affecting her.

There was no guile in her. It wasn't her style. If he
told her again to forget it, or something similar, then she
would have to accept it. But there was always the chance

that he might have changed his mind and her heartbeat quickened at the thought.

He was chatting to the man behind the counter now and she looked around her disinterestedly. There was a block of flats beside the garage, and as she observed them the glass in the window of an apartment on the first floor shattered and smoke started to belch forth.

'It's on fire,' somebody shouted, and she was out of the car in a flash.

Zoey still had her uniform on and she reached inside and grabbed the helmet which was lying on the back seat. Then she was running. Flinging herself towards the entrance of the flats.

'Dial 999,' she told the woman on the pavement who'd alerted everyone to what was happening, and in she went. There was a lift with a sign that said it was out of order, and as Zoey raced up a badly lit staircase doors on the landing above were opening and shrill voices asking what was the matter.

The door of the nearest flat was wide open and a woman was banging frantically on a door at the other end of a cluttered living room.

When Zoey burst in the woman cried, 'Thank God you're here! It's my lad, Connor. He's got fireworks in there. They've gone off and set the place on fire and he's got the door locked.'

Taking in the situation at a glance, Zoey banged on the door and bellowed, 'Open the door, Connor. Now!'

'I can't,' he cried in a muffled voice. 'That's where the fire is.'

'We're going to have to break it down,' Zoey told his terrified mother. 'You'll have to help me. If two of us put our shoulder against it, we might manage it.'

They tried but it didn't budge, and behind it the crackling of the fire was getting louder.

'The air coming in through the shattered window will be making the fire burn faster,' Zoey gasped. 'He's going to have to get out that way.'

'Where's the rest of your lot?' the other woman cried. 'Can't they put ladders up to take him down?'

'They're not here yet,' Zoey told her. 'I'm off duty. I was on the garage forecourt and—'

'Clear the building immediately,' she heard Alex telling the bewildered tenants on the landing, and then he was there, cool, calm and the most welcome sight she'd ever seen.

'Get out of here fast,' he told the woman, adding to Zoey, 'Find me a wet cloth to cover my face.'

As the boy's mother hesitated, Zoey ushered her out. 'Do as he says. We know what we're doing.'

There was a pile of ironing on the kitchen table. Grabbing a couple of towels, Zoey soaked them under the tap and ran back to where Alex had just put his shoulder to the door and had it creaking on its hinges.

He did it again. This time it flew open and with the blast of air that it created, flames and smoke came leaping outwards.

Alex moved back, but only for a second. Then with a towel over his nose and mouth he went in with Zoey close behind him.

'Go back!' he bellowed. 'You have no breathing apparatus.'

'Neither have you,' she said grimly, and followed him into the thick black smoke.

After groping around for precious seconds, they found the boy lying in a crumpled heap in the far corner of the room. Alex bent swiftly and heaved him over his shoulder.

'Come on!' he cried. 'Let's get out of here before the whole place goes up. You first, Zoey. I don't want to have to come back in here looking for you.'

It wasn't a moment to argue, so she did as she was told.

When they got out into the open Alex laid the limp figure of the youth on the grass verge outside the flats and she dropped to her knees beside him.

She'd heard his mother screaming hysterically as they'd brought him out but it had barely registered. The lad was suffering from burns and smoke inhalation and they had no equipment to treat him with.

To her dismay she saw that there was no rising of the chest to indicate he was still breathing. There was no pulse or heartbeat either and she told Alex, who was asking urgently if anyone had phoned the emergency services. 'He's gone! I'm about to resuscitate.'

'Right!' he said briskly. 'Let's see if we can bring him back. In the meantime, pray that help isn't long in coming or we're going to have one dead boy and the whole block of flats on fire.'

It could have only been seconds yet it seemed like a lifetime before paramedics were spilling out of an ambulance and the wail of a fire-engine siren indicated that colleagues from a station other than their own had arrived.

In those brief moments the boy began to breathe again and his mother, who had now relapsed into a shocked silence, grabbed Zoey's arm.

'It's OK,' Zoey told her quietly. 'We've got him back but he still needs urgent medical attention. Once he's in the ambulance they have oxygen and drugs to prevent any further cardiac arrest. They'll take over now.' As two paramedics fell to their knees beside the inert figure of the boy, she briefed them quickly and then got to her feet.

'Can you believe that just happened? That we were there when we were needed?' Alex shook his head and smiled wryly as, smoke-grimed and dishevelled, they set off for home once more. 'I didn't have to look far for you when I found the car empty.'

Zoey gave a tired smile. She was weary now after her exertions in the fire-engine 'pull' and the incident at the flats.

That sort of rescue had been a much more dangerous thing than when they had the back-up of the fire-engine's resources and other crew members to assist.

Luckily they'd been wearing their fireproof uniforms and helmets, but they'd had no breathing apparatus and now her throat felt raw and her eyes were smarting.

'You should have gone to Casualty, along with the boy, when the paramedics suggested it,' Alex said with a quick sideways glance at her blackened face.

'And what about you?' she parried. 'Isn't your throat dry and your eyes smarting?'

'Er…yes, but I'm not you. I don't want to see you suffering from smoke inhalation or any other nasty effects of the fire.'

'I'm all right,' she told him as her eyelids began to droop. 'A bath and a hot drink will put me right. I wish it were as simple for that foolish boy.'

'Yes. But remember he was still breathing and with the care he'll be getting now should make a full recovery.'

'If there's no brain damage,' she commented drowsily, and the next time Alex looked at her he saw she was asleep.

Zoey looked young and defenceless, slumped in the seat beside him, with the firm globes of her breasts rising and falling inside the bulky coat and her soft blonde hair tumbled over her face.

What was she doing in such a dangerous job? he asked himself irritably. Looking at her, he felt that she would look more at home in some kind of fashion out-let…and she'd certainly be at less risk there.

When she'd followed him into that kid's bedroom he'd wanted to bellow at her to obey orders. But they hadn't been on a fire-service 'shout'. It had been a one-off they'd stumbled on and he'd known that she wasn't going to take any notice of his command to stay out of it.

Fortunately she hadn't come to grief and a shudder went through him at the thought of how he would have felt if she had. He was getting involved, he told himself, and it was against his better judgement.

When her head slid sideways and came to rest against his shoulder, he turned and his lips brushed against her dishevelled golden bob.

She smelt of smoke. Not the most appealing of per-fumes. Yet it made his blood warm. He smiled. This confident young creature would run a mile if she dis-covered that she evoked a tenderness in him that made him want to take care of her. The knowledge really would widen the gap between them. She was more in the market for fun and romance.

Zoey was still asleep when he pulled up in front of Mandy's house and Alex sat looking down on her in the shadowed confines of the car. It seemed a shame to rouse her, but the autumn dusk was falling and he couldn't leave her there.

He touched her face gently and she murmured his name.

'Zoey,' he said gently. 'Time to wake up. We're home.'

'Hmm?'

'We're home, Zoey,' he repeated.

She opened her eyes and for a second gazed at him bewilderedly. Then she was straightening up in her seat and raking through her hair with a grubby hand.

'I can't believe I did that,' she groaned.

'What?'

'Went to sleep. What am I?'

'How about someone who's had a very busy day?'

'Mmm. I suppose so. We think that Rosie is teething so it doesn't help, being up in the middle of the night.'

'You mean to say that you've been up with the baby!' he exclaimed. 'Where was her mother?'

'We take turns.'

'But Mandy doesn't have a job.'

'I know, but I am here to help her. She's had a rough time.'

'And you haven't?'

Zoey's smile was wistful.

'Don't start on that again, Alex. Self-pity doesn't suit me.' And because she couldn't resist it, she asked, 'Do you remember last time?'

Did he remember! It had been those moments when he'd held her in his arms that were the cause of his present state of mind. He'd been quite content with his life before she'd appeared on the scene.

His marriage was over without any great amount of rancour on either side, to his great relief, and he'd been planning a woman-free existence. At least until such time as the taste of life with Gloria had left him.

But what had happened? Temptation had appeared in the form of a confident young blonde. Quite stunning in her own way and hardly likely to have the same outlook as a jaded divorcee like himself.

Zoey was waiting for a reply and as he looked into her wide sapphire gaze Alex knew he couldn't lie.

'Of course I remember,' he said stiffly, miffed that she was putting him on the spot like this. 'For some reason I feel that I have to look after you, though goodness knows why as you're one tough cookie.'

It was part of the truth, but not all of it. Alex hadn't told her that once she was in his arms he'd wanted to hold her for ever.

Her expression was telling him that he hadn't said what she wanted to hear and her next remark was in keeping with it.

'I don't need looking after, Alex,' she snapped. 'I've fended for myself since I was eighteen and haven't come to grief yet.'

It was on the tip of her tongue to tell him that there was something that she did need, but that it was connected with passion and desire, not the frailties associated with womankind.

Zoey reached out to open the car door and he knew he didn't want her to go.

'Let's go for a meal when we've washed and changed,' he said quickly. 'That's if you haven't anything else planned.' He gave a teasing smile. 'Or are you too tired?'

She beamed back at him, her temporary irritation banished at the thought of some more prime time together.

'I'd love to…and, no, I'm not tired.'

She would have gone if she'd been dropping in her tracks, she thought. But that short sleep in the car had pepped her up and now she couldn't wait to get inside and into something more alluring than her uniform.

'How long will it take you to get ready?' Alex asked, casual now that he'd managed to prolong their time together.

'An hour?'

'Fine. I'll come across and get you.'

'Zoey!' Mandy exclaimed when she saw her. 'Where've you got all the grime from? I thought it was a pleasure day today.'

'It was…is,' Zoey trilled from halfway up the stairs. 'The grime is from a fire that Alex and I got caught up in on our way home. But the rest of the day has been great and it isn't finished yet. We're going out for a meal.'

'Just the two of you?'

'Mmm.'

'Where to?'

'I don't know. He's the one who knows where to dine out in this area. I don't care where we go…just as long as he's there. What about you?' she asked. 'Is Harry coming round?'

Her stepmother pulled a face.

'Hardly. It's Saturday night, don't forget. But he's taking Rosie and me for a drive tomorrow afternoon, which will be nice.'

As Zoey lay soaking in perfumed water, she was deciding what to wear and smiling as the choice presented itself. It was always a temptation to wear black, but tonight there was the urge in her to dazzle. To let Alex see that amongst the other things that she was, trauma technician and child-minder, she was beautiful in her own special way.

There was a long sleeveless dress in her wardrobe that was the same colour as her eyes. It was plain and understated and yet the moment she put it on everything about her sprang to life. Hair, skin, curving slenderness, the lot.

What effect would it have on Alex? she wondered as she lifted a leg high out of the water and surveyed her toes. Would the day end how she wanted it to?

Don't bank on it, she told herself. He's picking up the pieces after Gloria. The ex-wife who is at present back in the marital home.

She would love to know why. Maybe now that she hadn't got Alex she wanted him back. If that was the case, she should have held onto him when she had him.

'Wow!' Mandy said when she saw her. 'Alex won't be able to take his eyes off you when he sees you in that.'

'I hope you're right,' Zoey sparkled. 'But I feel that he doesn't know what to make of me. Do you know, he didn't want me to be there as back-up when he went into the bedroom where the fire was at those flats? What do you think of that?'

Mandy's face was solemn.

'I can understand that.'

'You can?'

'Yes. You weren't on duty for one thing, and for another neither of you had breathing apparatus.'

'So what difference does it make?'

'I take it that he doesn't fuss when you're out on a call with the fire crew?'

'Er…no. Well, not much anyway.'

'Right. So you were both taking a big risk when you

brought that boy out to safety. Alex wouldn't have wanted your life to be on his conscience. Surely you see that.'

'Yes, but I was first on the scene.'

At that moment the doorbell rang and her stepmother said laughingly, 'Just for once let him be protective if he wants to.'

Alex's step had been light as he'd gone upstairs to shower, but before he'd been able to strip off a voice from down below had brought him to a halt.

'I've just got back from the hospital,' Gloria had said. 'Aunt Mary's surgery is scheduled for Monday.'

He'd looked down at her in some disbelief. For a moment he'd forgotten that she was back on the scene, but not for long. There was a trying time ahead for both Gloria and her elderly aunt and he would do what he could to make it easier. Even though her being back in his life was totally unexpected.

So he said gravely, 'I see. Well, let's hope that it all goes well for the old lady. And now, if you'll excuse me, Gloria, I need a shower. Zoey and I got involved in a fire of all things on the way home and I feel decidedly smoke-blackened.'

'What's going on between you and her?' Gloria asked in her flat legal voice.

Alex sighed. He didn't think for a moment that she was really interested.

'Nothing. We're just getting to know each other. Why do you ask?'

She shrugged.

'No reason. Just curious. She doesn't look your type.'

Alex frowned, irritated that Gloria felt in a position to comment. *She* hadn't been his type. Had she forgotten that?

When Zoey opened the door to him the frown was still there, and she took a step back.

'Ready?' he asked briefly.

She nodded, her bright expectations dimming.

'Yes,' she told him with like brevity, and without wasting any time settled herself into the passenger seat of his car.

'I thought we'd go to the local golf club if that's all right with you,' he said in a lighter tone as they pulled out onto the main road that ran past the fire station. 'The food's excellent.'

'Fine,' she said abruptly, thinking that if she'd dressed in an old sugar sack he couldn't have taken less notice of her.

Alex took his gaze off the road for a second.

'What's wrong, Zoey?'

'Nothing! Nothing at all!'

'Really? Well, I wouldn't like to see you when there is. How can you sit there looking so beautiful and yet be so miserable?'

'Me miserable! I beg your pardon. When I opened the door to you it was like when we first met. You were abrupt and monosyllabic. What have I done?'

'You haven't done anything,' he said levelly. 'If that's how I was, I'm sorry. Gloria was there when I got in, asking questions.'

'So she's still with you?' Zoey said flatly.

'Yes. An elderly aunt of hers is to undergo surgery and she's come to give moral support.'

It was none of her business but she had to ask.

'So how long is she staying?'

'I don't know. As long as it takes, I suppose. She's very close to the old lady and is in some distress.'

'So why didn't you ring me and cancel our arrangement?' Zoey said coolly. 'It would seem that you had more important things to do.'

'Like what?'

'Holding Gloria's hand. You were the first person she came to. Couldn't she stay at her aunt's house?'

'Hardly. She's in a rest home for the elderly.'

Zoey knew she was being unkind but she couldn't bear the thought of Alex being in such close intimacy with his ex-wife.

He was observing her set expression and he said levelly, 'I'm not taking you back. I asked you out for a meal and that is what we're going to do...eat...together...because we've earned it. OK?'

Zoey shrugged as if she couldn't care either way.

'Suit yourself. Just as long as you're not going to be pining to be back home all the time.'

'As if!' He was smiling and her spirits lifted when he went on to say, 'I haven't told you how fabulous you look.'

Not entirely forgiving him, she said, 'Don't follow that comment with the old cliché about how somebody will be a lucky fellow one day.'

'Why not?'

'Because it doesn't apply. I was supposed to be steering clear of love affairs after dating a firefighter who, unknown to me, was sleeping with one of the teachers we'd met during our talks to the schools.'

'And?'

'Oh, for goodness' sake, Alex. Stop pretending that you don't know what I mean.'

'You're crazy,' he said softly. 'I have no intention of

starting another relationship so soon after my divorce. It wouldn't be fair to all concerned.'

Zoey was sitting bolt upright in her seat.

'Including Gloria?'

'Maybe. The divorce wasn't all that long ago.'

'I see.'

He shook his head.

'No, you don't, Zoey. I'm trying to be sensible, if you'll let me.'

He was stopping the car in front of a spacious single-storey building on the edge of parkland, and as she observed him with mutinous eyes Alex said, 'Well? Are you ready to be wined and dined? Let's just concentrate on that, shall we? Enjoy each other's company and forget the rest.'

'All right,' she agreed, with a sinking feeling that if he could put something as serious as her feelings for him to one side so easily, there couldn't be much of a flame burning in return.

But as they were shown to a table Zoey was bouncing back. Why spoil the night with dismal thoughts? If Alex had any doubts about their budding relationship she was going to banish them here and now. She'd wanted to dazzle...and dazzle she would. Even though he had let his ex-wife back into the fold.

CHAPTER FOUR

ALEX watched Zoey with a quizzical smile as the meal progressed. She was obviously out to charm him, with eyes bright and mouth curving into laughter as she regaled him with amusing stories about happenings at the city-centre fire station where she'd worked before.

She talked about life with Mandy and Rosie, too, and it was all upbeat. No mention of the sadness and worry of the time when Mandy hadn't been coping very well and she'd been frantic about Rosie's well-being to the extent that she'd spent every free second with them.

She could discuss it light-heartedly now, as everything was so much better since she'd gone to live with them and Mandy had met Harry who owned the pizzeria. Nothing might come of it, but if having a man friend was making her young stepmother feel less desolate, it had to be good.

When she finally lapsed into silence Zoey sat twirling a wineglass between finger and thumb. She was leaning forward, watching Alex from beneath lowered lids. Alex could see the cleft between her firm, creamy breasts. Her perfume was as tantalising as before.

He was crazy if he thought he was going to resist Zoey Lawrence, he told himself. Intimate meetings of this sort weren't going to keep them out of each other's arms.

'I know what you're up to, you know,' he said in a low voice.

As she slowly raised her head and fixed him with her

challenging sapphire gaze, he called the waiter across to settle the bill. Once that was done he got to his feet. 'Let's go,' he said.

When they reached the shadows outside Alex stopped, and as she turned to face him he reached out and took her in his arms.

'You don't have to put yourself out to attract me,' he murmured against the smooth brightness of her hair. 'You're as enticing in the clumsy gear we wear for work as in this beautiful blue dress.'

'So?' she challenged.

'So this,' he said softly, and like a thirsty man who'd found an oasis he bent his mouth to hers and kissed her.

His lips were firm and warm...and demanding. His arms where she wanted them to be, around her. And his arousal, which she could feel hard against her own inner thighs, was making the moment complete.

This is it, Zoey thought dizzily. Love! We might have only known each other a few weeks, but it's as if I've always known Alex...and he me.

She was presuming too much. Even as the sentiments formed themselves in her mind, Alex was putting her gently away from him.

'I knew it was crazy to bring you out here,' he said with a sigh. 'I should have had more sense. I'm going to take you home, Zoey, before our feelings get the better of us.'

There was no teasing challenge in her eyes now. They were sparking fire.

'What's the matter?' she snapped. 'Have you just remembered there's someone waiting for you at home? Better the devil you know?'

Alex shook his head ruefully.

'You see. You're all upset now. We should have stayed as we were...friendly acquaintances.'

'You have some nerve!' she cried. 'I told you to take me back home in the first place. But you insisted on bringing me here. What had you in mind? The best of both worlds. A quick flirt with me and then back home to Gloria?'

'If that were the case we would have been further along the seduction line by now,' he protested tightly. 'I wouldn't have been considering your best interests.'

'Huh!' she snorted. 'I'll be the judge of what are my best interests...and now...yes...I would like to go home. I can't think of anything I would prefer more.'

They were both silent on the way back and when Alex pulled up in front of their respective houses Zoey was out of the car in a flash.

'Goodnight. Thanks for the meal,' she said stonily. As he would have spoken, she added, 'I don't want to hear it, Alex.'

On that parting note she walked up the drive with head held high and spirits as low as the hem of the blue dress around her ankles.

After Saturday night's dampener Sunday was a no-day as far as Zoey was concerned. She helped Mandy with household chores, did some lukewarm tidying up in the garden and was leaving the house with Rosie in her pram when she saw Gloria coming out of the house across the way.

She averted her head, having nothing to say to her, but irritatingly Gloria caught her up as she pointed the pram towards the main road. Of Alex there was no sign.

'You're the girl from the fire station, aren't you?' Gloria said as she drew level.

'Yes.'

'And you have a child, I see.'

'The baby isn't mine.'

'Oh. Whose is it?'

'Rosie is my stepsister.'

'Rather a big age gap.'

'That's right.'

Suddenly Zoey felt ashamed. She had no quarrel with this woman. No need to be so abrupt. It wasn't Gloria's fault that she was falling in love with her ex-husband.

'I'm turning off here,' she said, forcing a smile. 'Nice to have met you again.'

It wasn't strictly true but she had to say something to get away from her, but Gloria didn't seem to have any particular destination in view.

'I might as well do the same,' she said. 'I've come out mainly for some fresh air. Alex would have come with me but he'd arranged to go to hospital to visit some young fellow who was in a car crash on the hill road.'

And so why have you latched onto me? Zoey thought. We hardly know each other.

Daylight was fading. Another chilly autumn evening was approaching and when a car pulled up at the side of them and the driver opened the door on the passenger side, Gloria perked up.

'Hello, there, ladies,' Greg said. 'Anyone fancy a trip to the cinema?'

Zoey shook her head.

'No, thanks. As you can see, I've got my hands full.'

'How about you, Gloria?'

'Er…yes…why not?' she said. 'I spend most of my time visiting my aunt. It will make a nice change.'

'Absolutely,' Zoey agreed, with a fervour that

stemmed from a mixture of surprise and relief. She turned the pram and headed for home.

As she walked the last few yards back to the house she was wondering why it couldn't have been Alex wanting to walk with her instead of Gloria. But that wasn't likely after her snappy farewell of the night before, was it?

Another thought presented itself. What would Alex have to say when he discovered that Gloria had gone to the cinema with the smooth-tongued Greg?

When Alex saw Gloria fall in step beside Zoey he groaned. The two women in his life out for a stroll together!

One of them should by now be in the past, yet she wasn't. And the other? Beautiful Zoey. Like a proud young colt. Confident and outspoken when it came to what she wanted.

And what was wrong with that? He ought to be over the moon that she wanted him. But he'd rushed into marriage once. Not given it enough thought. It wasn't going to happen again.

As they disappeared round the corner of the cul-de-sac he got into his car. He was committed to visiting the lad in hospital, and a promise made was a promise kept as far as he was concerned. But he would have dearly liked to know what sort of a conversation Zoey and Gloria were having.

When Zoey turned up at the station on Monday morning Geoff said, 'We've got a suggestion.'

There were smiles all round and a few nudges and she observed them warily.

'Oh, yes?'

'Yeah. The guy that you replaced used to be the morale officer. He kept us cheerful when things weren't so good. It's hard not to be affected when there's been a "shout" and there are bodies to be brought out of a burning building or untangled from what's left of a car.

'It's happened to all of us at one time or another and we don't always manage to get it in perspective. But if one of the team is there to do a bit of counselling and cheering up, it can make a lot of difference to whether we sleep at night.'

'And so what are you saying?' she asked slowly.

'That you take his place, Zoey. Even on a normal day, just looking at you makes us feel better. What do you say?'

'I'd like to know what Alex thinks first.'

'It was his suggestion.'

'Really?'

That was surprising! Especially as she was in just as much need of cheering up as anyone at the moment. Maybe he thought that if she had to spread herself around a bit more, she would forget her fixation about him.

'All right, I'll do it,' she agreed. 'Just as long as I don't end up being a perpetual hand-holder or shoulder to cry on. Or...' with a mischievous glance at Alex who'd just come out of the office '...asked to organise sing-songs.'

She was making a joke of it, but she knew that there were times when the impersonality that the emergency services strove for to keep them sane fell apart in times of great stress, and a calm word or a friendly gesture could make all the difference.

At that moment she had no means of knowing that in the very near future the morale of the fire crew would be at its lowest ebb.

It was Friday afternoon and the end of a long and uneventful week. Zoey was feeling restless and on edge and had thought a few times that the role of morale-booster might be sitting on the wrong shoulders.

She would have felt better if Alex had made some mention of their brief passionate encounter outside the golf club, but he was putting up a barrier of bland politeness between them and, still sore at the way she'd been brought down to earth so abruptly, she'd decided that if that was how he wanted it to be, it was all right by her.

Yet if there was pretence between them now, she knew that it hadn't been like that when he'd held her in his arms and they'd leapt to answer each other's need.

There had been wonder in the moment. A magic unlike anything she'd ever experienced before. And what had he done? Cheapened it into a casual encounter.

She'd caught him watching her a few times with a sort of guarded thoughtfulness and it had taken all her time not to go up to him and demand that they talk it through.

Yet something always held her back. Pride? Uncertainty? She didn't know, as now she wasn't the confident person that he'd described her as.

If Mandy had noticed that she was in the doldrums, she hadn't commented. Her own life was coming together again because of her friendship with Harry, and as she began to sparkle so Zoey's zest faltered.

The 'shout', when it came in the last hour of Friday's shift, was for engine and crew to turn out to a blaze in the science laboratory at the nearby comprehensive school, attended by some of the older children of the firefighters.

A police presence was already on the scene when they got there, and after having a quick word with the officer in charge Alex told them in their own familiar jargon, 'It's a persons reported. We don't know how many. Most of the pupils and staff had gone home when there was an explosion in the lab. But there were still one or two stragglers on the premises and the head teacher and caretaker were seen running in this direction. Neither of them have been seen since.'

While he was speaking they'd been attaching the hoses and donning breathing apparatus and were almost ready to go into the single-storey building where the blaze was.

'We don't know what caused the explosion,' the police officer told them tersely. 'There might be another if the fire spreads to other equipment.'

'Great!' one of the men said dolefully. 'That's all we need, with gas taps all over the place. It'll have been kids messing about. You'll see.'

The school's laboratory was much bigger inside than they'd expected, and as the fire crew groped their way through the dense smoke and rising flames Alex was in the forefront, with Zoey and the others close behind.

'Spread out,' he called over his shoulder, and almost fell over the body of a woman lying at his feet.

Zoey was by his side in a flash and she saw immediately that the disappearance of the headmistress had been solved. Who would they find next?

There was no time to ponder on that score. They were bringing her out, and if the ambulance services hadn't yet arrived, she would be needed to treat the woman...if it wasn't too late.

It seemed that it might be. When they laid her down at a safe distance from the burning building Zoey found that there was no heartbeat or pulse. The woman's lips were blue, her skin cold and clammy, and as Zoey desperately tried to resuscitate her it became clear that the headmistress had suffered a cardiac arrest as she'd run into the building to check that none of her pupils were inside.

Paramedics were on the scene now and as it became obvious that life was not going to return to the still form in front of them, their faces were sombre.

As Zoey got slowly to her feet, Alex and the others were bringing out the caretaker and a teenage boy. The youth was badly burned, the man suffering from smoke inhalation. As if the moment wasn't horrendous enough, Alex told her tightly, 'It's Geoff's lad. We found him by one of the workbenches.'

'Oh, no!' Zoey breathed. 'How awful! Where is Geoff?'

'Over there, vomiting. He was the one who found him.'

The ambulance crews had taken over the casualties. One lot were giving the caretaker oxygen and the others preparing to wrap the injured youth in a water gel blanket to stop the skin tightening before they got him to the burns unit.

Geoff was beginning to absorb the shock of finding his son in the lab and was now hurrying to be by his side.

'I never expected this,' he said hoarsely as he prepared to board the ambulance that was taking the lad to hospital. He cast an anguished look at the still form of the headmistress. 'Dead?'

'Afraid so,' Alex told him.

Geoff groaned.

'That woman lived for the school.'

'And now she's died for it,' Zoey said quietly. 'Let's pray that she's the only one.'

The rest of the men were working to get the blaze under control now that the casualties had been brought out, and the atmosphere was grim.

It was one of their own close-knit band who was suffering from the results of this fire, and as most of them had children of their own, they could comprehend what Geoff was going through.

'Let me tell Geoff's wife,' Alex told the police. 'She'll take it better from one of us. They live right next to the station, so as soon as we get back one of us will take her to hospital.'

It was late that night and Zoey had been on edge ever since arriving home. Alex had left them abruptly while they'd been putting the engine away and had gone to see Mrs Baines.

Within seconds she'd seen his car set off for the hospital with an ashen-faced woman in the passenger seat, and ever since then she'd been waiting for news.

It came at last. At eleven o'clock he rang the doorbell and her first words as she let him in were, 'How's the boy?'

He looked tired, drawn, and had no smiles for her.

'Lost the sight of one eye. Has second-degree burns down one side of his face and on the upper arm that he tried to shield himself with.'

Zoey shook her head sadly.

'Do we know what happened?'

'Yes. Geoff's kid sneaked back after the chemistry lesson to try out an experiment of his own. He was too ill to be properly interviewed, but they did manage to get that out of him.'

'And his parents?'

'What do you think? Devastated.'

She pointed to the sofa.

'Sit down and I'll make you a drink.'

'I won't say no to that,' he said, doing as she'd suggested. 'I'm desperate for a wash and a change of clothes, but those sort of needs seem very unimportant after today's tragedies. That poor woman…Geoff's son…and the caretaker.

'He's come out of it the best of the three. The staff and governors of the school are dumbstruck at what has happened to the head. No one can believe it.'

He yawned and raked his hand tiredly through his dark locks, and by the time Zoey appeared from the kitchen with a steaming mug of hot chocolate he was asleep.

She stood looking down at him tenderly. 'Action man' had given in to human frailty. It was nice to see his vulnerable side for once.

She bent and planted a gentle kiss on his brow. His eyes flew open and she sighed. She should have known better than think that he had really succumbed to weariness.

Reaching out for the drink, he patted the cushions beside him and said, 'Where's Mandy?'

'Out with the new man in her life.'

'You mentioned she had someone—what's his name?'

'He's called Harry and I told you, he owns the local pizzeria. I can hear wedding bells in the distance.'

'Really?' he said, sitting up straighter. 'So that would leave you free to get on with your own life?'

'Er…yes…I suppose so. I hadn't given it much

thought. Though I might have done if a certain person hadn't been so touch-me-not.'

'Me?'

'Who else?'

He put the mug down and turned towards her.

'And you think it's easy…resisting you.'

'It must be. You seem cheerful enough.'

'There's cheerful…and cheerful, Zoey. I haven't felt really light-hearted in years.'

'I've not been exactly on top of the world myself since Dad died,' she said quietly. 'Before that I was having a great time—lots of friends, parties, theatres, the lot—but it all went by the board when I saw the state Mandy was in.'

Her voice thickened.

'I've been so lonely, with no one to turn to, and…'

The words trailed away into silence as she thought, What am I doing? Asking for sympathy again! Alex will think I'm a veritable Miss Whinge.

He put his arm around her shoulders and cuddled her up against him.

'So we're both putting on an act,' he said, with his chin resting on the golden crown of her head. 'Crazy, aren't we? There is a difference, though. Once your stepmother is settled again with someone who cares for her, the way ahead will be clear for you. While I have the legacy of a failed marriage to contend with and an ex-wife who has appeared on the scene again.'

As Zoey swivelled round to face him their eyes were only inches apart.

'So what?' she exclaimed. 'Gloria need only be a problem if you let her. It seems strange to me that she didn't find somewhere else to stay if she wanted to come back here, instead of planting herself on you. If you had nothing in common before, you must have even less now...unless you're both having second thoughts.

'And as for having a failed marriage, so what? Failed...gone...kaput...none of that matters as long as you don't let it spoil things for us.' Her voice had softened. 'Because we are right for each other, aren't we, Alex?'

He wanted to resist the appeal in the sapphire eyes looking into his. Ignore the mouth that was parted in anticipation of the reply that she was begging for. Clamp down on the longing that was making his loins ache. Yet he did none of those things.

When he kissed the mouth that was made for his kisses, and felt the soft mounds of her breasts harden at his touch, reason was a far-away thing, something for others to indulge in. To make love to Zoey Lawrence would be like coming in out of the cold.

A car pulling up on the drive outside brought an end to that fantasy.

'Oh, no!' Zoey breathed. 'Mandy's back. Let's go across to your place.'

He shook his head.

'I've got Gloria staying with me, don't forget.'

'So? She doesn't sleep in your bed, does she?'

Alex was getting to his feet.

'You should know better than to ask that kind of question.'

'In other words, you don't want to answer it,' she said with sudden weariness. 'Mandy coming home has provided you with an escape route. You'll be able to look yourself in the eye tomorrow, knowing that you didn't succumb to the bimbo in the house across the way.'

'I ought to smack your backside for that remark,' he said grimly. 'If Mandy hadn't come back when she did, you might at this moment be regretting losing your virginity. That is, supposing it hasn't already been lost.'

'Yes! Quite so! And that is something for me to know and for you to find out…one day when you've sorted out your affairs.'

'Hello, Alex. Nice to see you.' Mandy was framed in the doorway and he forced a smile.

'Nice to see you, too,' he told her. Ignoring Zoey's stormy gaze, he went on, 'Have you had a pleasant evening?'

'Lovely, thanks. What have you folks been up to?'

'Not a lot,' he said levelly. 'I've been at the hospital most of the evening, giving support to one of the fire crew whose son has been badly burnt. I called here on my way back to let Zoey know how the lad was, and she offered me…er…sustenance.'

Very funny, Zoey thought. They both knew what had been on offer and it hadn't just been a mug of hot chocolate. But he'd reminded her again of the sort of day he'd had and, though Alex had only dozed for a matter of minutes, he must be tired.

So getting off the sofa to stand beside him, she chucked him playfully under the chin and said airily, 'Off you go, then, or your ex will be sending out a search party.'

He laughed, and called her bluff, remarking, 'Gloria will have a pretty good idea where I am, but I will go. It's been a long and trying day.'

When he'd gone Mandy said, 'You seem very perky.'

Zoey groaned.

'Don't you believe it. It would be easier to charm the fish out of the sea than get through to that one.'

In the week that followed Zoey found that spirits at the station were very low, as was to be expected. There had been a post-mortem on the much-respected headmistress, and to no one's surprise the cause of death had been diagnosed as cardiac failure.

The funeral was to take place on the coming Saturday and some of the men at the fire station and their families would be attending.

Geoff's son was still very poorly in the burns unit, but the caretaker had been discharged from hospital. That was the only good thing that had happened since the explosion in the school laboratory.

The lad's distraught parents didn't know whether charges would be brought against their son, but right now it wasn't their main concern.

Given the task of boosting morale in a situation such as the present one, Zoey did her best to put on a cheerful front, but it wasn't easy. The men were all friends. They spent a lot of their free time together, as well as their working hours, and when one of them hurt they all hurt.

It seemed as if Alex had once more put their brief moment of bliss into his file of events to be forgotten. He was pleasant, polite, but far from personal whenever they were in each other's company.

'In some ways I don't feel old enough to be offering counsel to the men,' she told Dorothea the cleaner one afternoon when there'd been more gloom than usual.

'Don't be thinking that,' the older woman said. 'Only this morning one of them was saying that just looking at you cheers them up. Alex is the one I worry about. There's no domestic joy in his life, and here at work he carries everybody's burdens.'

Zoey felt shame wash over her. It was true, and all she had been bothered about were her own plans and desires. The next time they were alone together, if that day ever dawned, she would admit to being a selfish little beast.

Greg was still hovering whenever he got the chance, and Zoey wished he wouldn't. He wasn't her type for one thing, and for another she felt he wasn't cut out for the job.

That was until the morning when they'd been called to a house fire and as it had been a persons reported emergency she'd been one of those searching a rambling old house for possible casualties.

There hadn't been any and she'd turned to grope her way outside when a smouldering beam had fallen and a glancing blow to the shoulder had sent her flying. Greg had been behind her and he'd picked her up and half carried her out of the building.

She'd been shaken by the incident and had let her rescuer hold her longer than had been necessary. When Alex had hurried over to ask if she was all right she'd said, 'Yes, thanks to Greg.' And had flashed the man in question a grateful smile.

It had been a mistake, being too effusive. For the rest of the day he'd hinted that he wouldn't mind seeing her gratitude in a more practical form.

So while Alex had been carrying out his duties tight-lipped and withdrawn, the station Romeo had been doing his best to get her to agree to meeting him that evening.

Zoey had shaken her head and used Mandy and Rosie as her excuse when she'd told him, 'I've too many family commitments at the moment, Greg. Maybe when the baby is older.'

'Suit yourself,' he'd said with surly brevity. 'I know that it's Carradine that you're after.'

'I'm not ''after'' anybody,' she'd flared. 'You make me sound like some sort of scalp hunter.'

'So?' he'd taunted, and she'd decided that enough was enough where Greg Osbourne was concerned.

The funeral of the teacher was over and there was better news about Geoff's son. He would need skin grafts and would have to cope with the loss of an eye, but his general condition was improving. So much so that his father reported for duty on Monday morning.

With his appearance the atmosphere lightened and Zoey gave a sigh of relief. It hadn't been easy keeping up morale, especially as she wasn't feeling on top of the world herself.

But she'd reasoned that being kept at arm's length by the man she was falling in love with was as nothing compared to Geoff's problems and those of the head-mistress's family.

Yet it didn't stop her from fretting inwardly, especially as Gloria's stay with Alex seemed to be going on for ever.

Dark November had replaced a mild October and Zoey wasn't the only one thinking that Gloria was outstaying her welcome. Her aunt had come through the operation satisfactorily but was now very frail and had been admitted to a smaller hospital for post-operative care. Which meant that her niece was still visiting her on a regular basis.

Gloria didn't seem to have any concerns about being away from the law practice where she was employed, and if she was aware that Alex was finding her extended stay irksome she didn't do anything about it.

A few days had become a few weeks. Yet he couldn't just ask her to leave. As long as she was concerned about the old lady he would have to put up with having her around, but the moment her aunt was allowed back to the rest home he was going to suggest that she move out.

For one thing, the stalemate situation that he'd created between Zoey and himself wasn't going to resolve itself with Gloria around. He reckoned that most folk would think it a funny set-up, he and Gloria back together.

Feeling drained and dispirited after a stressful day at the fire station, Zoey was making her way home on a cold winter night when she saw Gloria getting out of her car outside Alex's house.

So the limpet was still in residence, she thought glumly. There had to be a spark of some kind left from their marriage for Alex to put up with her prolonged presence like he was doing.

As she watched the other woman unloading shopping from the boot of the car, there was the sound of running feet and to Zoey's horror she saw a dark figure make a grab at the handbag over Gloria's shoulder.

She screamed and tried to fight him off but he was determined. Without having to think twice, Zoey threw herself across the road and jumped on him from behind.

With an angry roar he left hold of the bag and, turning, he pushed her off him, sending her crashing to the ground. Then he was running off down the road empty-handed, leaving Gloria still screaming hysterically and Zoey horizontal on the pavement with the breath knocked out of her.

As she struggled to a sitting position Alex's voice cried from above, 'Zoey! What's happened?'

As he bent over her she saw horror on his face in the light of the streetlamps. 'Are you hurt?' he asked urgently.

'No. At least I don't think so,' she gasped. 'See to Gloria. She was being robbed and I came across to help fight him off.'

His ex-wife's screams had turned to sobs.

'So what happened, Gloria?' he asked, putting his arms around her.

'I'd just come home from shopping,' she wailed, 'and as I was taking the stuff out of the boot this fellow came up from behind and tried to take my bag.'

'Did you recognise him?'

'Er…no. It was too dark.'

'I saw a guy running along the road as I turned out of the fire-station car park,' he said grimly. 'I guess that would be him. He wouldn't have got far if I'd known what he'd been up to.'

Zoey was standing to one side, watching them. Her face hurt where she'd hit the ground with such force, but what hurt even more was the feeling that Gloria looked as if that was where she belonged…in Alex's arms.

He turned and as their eyes met in the dim light he said, 'Let's get you both inside. Zoey's taken a nasty fall.'

'I'm all right,' she said quickly. 'Mandy will be wondering where I am.'

He'd taken his arms away from Gloria and was propelling them both towards the house.

'You're coming inside with me first,' he said firmly. 'I want to check you over. Make sure there are no broken bones. Then you can phone Mandy. All right?'

She nodded meekly, too miserable to argue.

The side of her face was grazed from when she'd hit the ground and bruising was already showing. No doubt a black eye would be part of the aftermath. Her shoulder was also hurting where she'd fallen, and even before Alex suggested it she'd decided that a visit to A and E was required to make sure that nothing was broken.

Alex was very pale. They all were. But the skin of his face had a stretched look about it when he said, 'I'm going to take you to Casualty, Zoey.'

She thought, Surely he isn't looking like that because I ended up in a heap on the pavement?

'You can't leave me!' Gloria cried. 'He might come back.'

'That's not likely. He was a street mugger. Not Burglar Bill,' he told her tersely.

'Can't you just phone for an ambulance to take her?' she protested, still apprehensive, and Zoey had to smile, even though her lips were beginning to swell.

No thanks for coming to the rescue. She couldn't even refer to her by name. Gloria wanted Alex back in her life. Zoey could feel it in her bones.

'Certainly not,' he said levelly. 'If you're nervous, you'd better come with us.'

There were plenty of bruises but thankfully no broken bones, and when in shared relief Alex and Zoey returned to the waiting room at the hospital, they found Gloria drinking coffee and leafing through a magazine.

At that moment Zoey decided she'd had enough of Gloria. For one thing, she was ravenous, not having eaten since lunchtime. On top of that, she was aching from the fall. If Alex was prepared to put up with his ex-wife's lack of sensitivity, she wasn't. So, assuming a briskness that was far from real, she told them coolly, 'I'd like to go home now for some food and a good hot bath.'

'Of course,' he said with an anxious glance at her

swollen face. 'It makes me shudder when I think what he might have done to you. As it is, it's bad enough. Promise me that you'll take the painkillers that they've given you. And, Zoey...'

'What?'

'Don't report for duty tomorrow unless you feel up to it.'

She wished she didn't feel that Alex was following some sort of guidelines. She didn't doubt his concern, but after seeing Gloria in his arms she was finding it difficult to forget that he must have held her like that countless times before. Was it surprising if the bond was still there?

CHAPTER FIVE

MANDY had already eaten when Alex dropped Zoey off at the house, and she exclaimed, 'Are you all right? I was worried when I got your phone call. What an awful thing to happen.'

Her eyes widened and her brown ponytail swung to and fro as she shook her head in horror at the sight of the grazes on Zoey's face.

'So tell me?' she cried. 'What happened?'

'I was on the point of coming inside when I looked across and saw Alex's wife being attacked outside the house.'

Mandy was positively goggling now and she glanced uneasily behind her.

'And you got involved?' was her next question.

'Yes. I couldn't not do, could I? I jumped on his back and he knocked me to the ground and ran off.'

'What was he like?' Mandy asked fearfully.

Zoey shrugged aching shoulders.

'I don't know. I only saw him from the back.'

Her stepmother shuddered.

'Did you report it to the police?'

She shook her head. 'No. There seemed no point. None of us saw him properly and he didn't get away with anything. I would imagine that people are reporting those sorts of incidents all the time. Gloria was very shaken, which isn't surprising, but Alex arrived soon after and was there to offer comfort.'

For once in her life she'd wished that she was a clinging vine instead of an independent woman. Then she might have been his first concern instead of the unglorious Gloria.

She ate a solitary meal with her mind still going over what had happened earlier. It had been the last thing she'd expected...or wanted...to be involved with both Alex and Gloria at the same time.

Him yes, but not her. Seeing them together had made her own hopes and longings seem futile. Before tonight his ex-wife's presence in his house had been just an irritating niggle. Now she saw it as a threat to all that she longed for. And unless she wanted to risk being told to mind her own business, there was nothing she could do about it.

Why didn't that woman go back to where she'd come from? She would volunteer to take over ministering to the elderly aunt herself if Gloria would do that.

Alex had said that Gloria had wanted to make a fresh start somewhere else when the divorce had come through and she had done so. But for some reason she was back in the fold. Had she had a change of mind? Was the sick relative angle just a ploy to be near him?

The moment they were back at the house, after dropping Zoey off, Alex turned to Gloria.

'You didn't exactly fall over yourself to thank Zoey for going to your assistance,' he said levelly.

'I don't know what you mean,' she protested.

'Oh, yes, you do. That fellow might have had a gun or a knife and one of you could have been injured or killed. She didn't have to get involved, you know. You behave as you do with her because you think I'm attracted to her, don't you?'

She eyed him coolly.

'Well, you are.'

He sighed. They'd known each other for so long he could almost read her mind.

'And what if I am? I didn't object to you going to the cinema with that smoothie Osbourne.'

'That was nothing.'

'Oh, no? Don't let's have one set of rules for me and another for you, Gloria. And while we're on the subject, how much longer are you going to be here?'

'Not much longer,' she said defiantly. 'You know that I had a very good reason for asking you to accommodate me.'

'Yes, that's true,' he agreed, 'and I'm going along with it, aren't I? But don't make life difficult for Zoey and myself.'

As Alex lay sleepless that night, he told himself that Gloria was just doing a bit of hanging on. She never had liked to lose anything that belonged to her, even though she'd raised no objection to the divorce.

But if she hadn't moved on, he had, and his thoughts turned to Zoey. Beautiful, brave Zoey.

He was accustomed to seeing her take risks. It was part of the job and he always wished her far away when danger was near, but the last thing he wanted to contemplate was her risking life and limb out on the street at the hands of some thug who was attacking Gloria.

If Zoey wished his ex-wife far away, he wished her even farther. He'd thought that once the divorce was through they would be out of each other's hair, but her prolonged presence was intruding into the new life he'd made for himself, and today's episode hadn't helped.

As his restlessness continued, he got up and went to the window. There was a light on at the house across the road so someone was still up, and a sudden desperate need to know that Zoey was all right overwhelmed him.

As he crossed the road Alex thought that he'd been pretty brusque with Gloria but sometimes he felt that he didn't know her at all and at others that he knew her only too well.

'Oh!' he exclaimed when Zoey opened the door to him. 'That really is a shiner. How are you feeling?'

'Unlovely and unloved,' she said wryly. 'Dare I hope that you've come to make me feel better?'

'I couldn't sleep,' he told her, 'and thought that if you were still up I'd come across to see how you were.'

'I was the same,' she said wearily. 'Tossing and turning.'

She had an old towelling robe on and her feet were bare. Her hair looked as if she'd washed it and just left it, as it lay flatly against her head like a lustreless cap. And with the black eye and its surrounding bruising providing a lurid range of colours, she was definitely not looking her best.

Yet she was lovely to him. There was something valiant and feisty about her. Those things, along with her slender golden fairness, made her the most desirable thing he'd ever seen.

As she stepped back to let him in, he said gently, 'Come here, my battered one.' Taking her in his arms, he touched her swollen face gently and told her, 'Don't ever expose yourself to such danger again. It's bad enough on the job, but thinking of you being at the mercy of some thug makes my blood run cold.'

'I know of a way to heat it up again,' she said laughingly. 'Shall I show you?'

He bent his mouth to hers.

'Like this, you mean?'

'Mmm. Just like that…except that it hurts.'

'I'm content to just hold you for as long as you'll let me,' he said softly.

She was smiling but there was a question in her eyes.

'What about Gloria, Alex?'

'What about her?'

'Is it really over between you?'

He sighed.

'Of course.'

'Then why is she living under your roof?'

'I thought I'd told you. She's here because of an elderly aunt who's had surgery. Staying at my place is convenient for visiting.'

'But it's been going on for weeks.'

'The recuperation is taking longer than expected.'

'I see. So you don't mind?'

'I'm prepared to put up with it if that's what you mean, as Gloria and I go back a long way.'

'Unlike ourselves.'

He'd been frowning, but now there was a glint of amusement in his glance.

'Yes…unlike ourselves.'

'Maybe that's why I feel I can't compete.'

'I'm not with you.'

'You know her through and through…and you don't know me at all.'

'And you think I'm unwilling to take a step into the unknown?'

'Yes. Something like that.'

'You'd be surprised how well I feel I know you, Zoey,' he said, back to being serious. 'Any reservations I might have come from somewhere else. The aftermath of divorce, for instance. Lots of people rush into marriage again the moment the divorce is through as if desperate to prove that they are desirable to someone, and often it leads to another catastrophe.'

'Well, thanks for that, Alex,' she said stiffly, moving away from him. 'I thought you'd come across to cheer me up. How wrong I was! So you see the way we feel about each other as the forerunner of a catastrophe. You're not the only one who's discovered that human relationships can be tricky. But they can also be fantastic when the two people concerned really love each other.

'Maybe you still care about Gloria as you seem loath to do anything to upset her. If that's the case, why don't you say so and I'll back off? It seems as if I'm always attracted to the wrong sort of men, those who have other women in their lives and find me all right for a bit of light relief. But when it comes to the crunch...'

Alex's jaw was tightening as he said, 'I would have thought you knew me better than that...and what's this about the ''wrong sort of men''? Who else are you referring to?'

Zoey tossed her head rebelliously, indignation still upon her.

'Why? Did you think you were the first?'

'It would appear that I was mistaken if I did,' he remarked drily. 'I'm just one of a string of conquests, am I?'

'I'm hardly likely to see you as that, am I?' she retaliated. 'You are the most unconquerable man I've ever met.'

He ignored that and in the same flat tone asked, 'And what happened to them all?'

'Oh, this and that,' she told him airily, while beginning to think dismally that in her pique she'd behaved like a spoilt child. Allowing Alex to believe that he was one of many when in truth there'd only been Damien the devious.

What was the matter with her? Was it jealousy? She wanted to throw herself back into his arms and tell him that it wasn't how she'd described it at all, but he was turning to go and she didn't blame him. With what was left of her dignity she picked up the skirt of her robe and began to climb the stairs.

Was anything ever simple? Alex asked himself as he went back to his own house. He didn't blame Zoey for getting worked up about what was going on.

It did look as if he was letting Gloria manipulate him, but although she was living in his house they were leading completely separate lives. The only physical contact they'd had had been when he'd held her in his arms after the attempted mugging, and Zoey seemed to have latched onto that as if it had meant something to him. She wasn't to know that his ex-wife got more satisfaction from reading a legal document than from a close embrace.

Hopefully she would soon depart and then he and Zoey could get to know each other better...explore their feelings. But he already knew how she felt. It was his own feelings that he was going to have to face up to.

As Zoey slipped beneath the bedcovers she was wishing she hadn't been so uptight with Alex. She'd questioned his integrity and made him sound indecisive where Gloria was concerned when she knew very well that he was the least indecisive person she'd ever met.

She had to admit that one reason why she'd been so indignant was because she was jealous of Gloria's place in his life. She was supposed to be part of his past, but she wasn't, was she? At the moment she was well and truly in the present.

Then there'd been the calm logic with which he'd explained his feelings about divorce and its aftermath, making her feel as if she never gave any serious thought to anything.

But Alex could be on the defensive as much as he liked, she thought wearily as she drifted into sleep. One thing he couldn't deny. He wanted her as much as she wanted him, and what had she done when he'd been full of protective concern for her? Berated him and then stalked off to bed. Leaving him to see himself out. If she wasn't careful, the man in her life would be telling her to grow up.

'So what happened to you?' the firefighters wanted to know when Zoey arrived at the station the next morning.

Alex was already there and she glanced at him quickly to see his expression. It was bland, giving nothing away, so she said casually, 'I fell on the pavement.'

It was the truth, but not all of it, and once the interest had died down she followed him into the office.

'I'm sorry about last night,' she said contritely. 'I was tired and aching all over. Do you forgive me?'

He smiled.

'Of course. I shouldn't have disturbed you at such a late hour. Let's forget it, shall we?'

'What, everything? The bit before I got ratty as well?'

'Yes. At least for the time being.'

'I see.'

He sighed.

'If only you did.'

At that moment the police came through to say they were needed at a house fire and the non-productive conversation came to an end.

With Bonfire Night in the past and Christmas approaching, the firework hazard was being replaced by candles. The crew had already been called out to a house fire where there'd been a party and much drinking had taken place. A candle that had been left burning had fallen over and set curtains alight.

Luckily no one had been hurt. Yet it was a warning that candlelit rooms were all very nice, but they could be the forerunner to disaster.

And now here was another house fire, stemming from the same kind of hazard but in very different circumstances. It wasn't the result of jollification. The householder had been using candles because the electricity supply had been cut off for non-payment.

On a gloomy morning in late November, small children playing in a downstairs room had caused a blaze by knocking a candle over onto sheets of paper that they'd been drawing on.

The mother, who had been gossiping with a neighbour at the front door, had sensibly whisked them to safety and then shut off the room until the fire-engine arrived, by which time the sparse furnishings were well alight.

When they got there it was bedlam, with the children screaming and the neighbour having hysterics. Only the young mother was calm and Zoey thought that she must be used to catastrophes. They'd already been living without light and now the house was on fire.

'Maybe they'll rehouse us now,' she said prosaically as she and her family gathered on the pavement. 'Don't be in any rush to put it out.'

'Sorry to disappoint you, but we've already damped

it down,' Alex told her as the hoses were turned off. 'You'll need to get in touch with Social Services. This place won't be fit to live in until it has dried out.'

The woman shrugged.

'It wasn't fit to live in before. They'll have to do something.'

'I'm sure they will,' he said, 'and, please, keep your children away from candles in future.'

As they drove back to the fire station Zoey thought that when they were working there was always harmony between Alex and herself. Possibly because they had the same amount of dedication and were part of a committed team. But away from it was a different matter.

They were deeply attracted to each other, no matter what Alex said to the contrary. Yet it always went wrong when they were alone. Maybe she should try to fix some prime time for them when there was no one else, such as Gloria, to command his attention.

The attempted mugging was still very much to the front of her mind. She wondered how Gloria was feeling today. More gracious, she hoped. The incident could have brought them closer, which could only have been a good thing.

It might have helped her to understand Alex's ex-wife better, as she would very much like to know what was going on in that one's mind. But it hadn't, and she couldn't help but think that, alarming as it had been, Gloria would rather it had been someone else who'd gone to her rescue.

Zoey had booked a day's leave the following week so that she could look after Rosie while Mandy and Harry went out on their own.

She waylaid Alex as they put the fire-engine away and

said casually, 'I'm minding the baby next Wednesday so that Mandy can have some time with Harry. Would you like to come for a meal?'

He stopped in his tracks, waited until the rest of the crew had gone inside and then said, 'What's the occasion?'

'There isn't one. Unless you would call us spending some time together an occasion.'

He looked down on her from the high metal step of the fire-engine and remarked, 'It will be if we can keep the peace.'

'So you'll come?'

'Yes. What time?'

'Half six?'

'Fine. And, Zoey…let it be just about us.'

Her smiled flashed out. 'That's the intention. Unless you want to bring Gloria along to make up a happy little threesome.'

He pursed his lips.

'No. I see enough of Gloria as it is.'

Greg was observing them from the station doorway and there was a knowing smile on his face.

'There's a phone call for you from Area Command,' he told Alex, 'if you can tear yourself away.'

When Alex had gone inside Zoey glowered at the messenger and Greg's smirk widened.

'Alex is back with his wife. You're wasting your time.'

'Really? Ex-wife, I think you mean. And I'll be the best judge of whether I'm wasting my time,' she said coolly, and pushed past him.

But once inside with a mug of hot tea in her hand, Zoey didn't feel so confident. Was what Greg had just said the general opinion, and she was the only one not facing up to it? Yet if that were the case, would Alex have agreed to her suggestion for the coming Wednesday?

She sighed and Geoff, who was seated nearby, said, 'What's dimming your light today, Zoey?'

'Oh, this and that,' she said with a pale smile, 'and none of it as depressing as what you're going through.'

He nodded.

'Yes, it's been a bad time for me and mine, but thankfully the lad is coping...and we've still got him. That's the main thing.'

December had arrived and with it the awareness that Christmas was approaching fast. Zoey expected that Mandy would be spending most of it with Harry, when he wasn't at the pizzeria. As for herself, she had no idea what she would be doing over the festive season.

Whether she enjoyed it or not would depend on the man who lived across the way. Their relationship would have to move on a bit if they were going to see anything of each other over the Christmas period.

But first, as a stepping stone, was the evening they were going to share. Once Rosie was tucked up in her cot the night would be theirs. Every time Zoey thought about it her eyes sparkled.

Alex would be working during the day while she was looking after Rosie and shopping for food, but once he'd been home to change they would be together.

She was no great cook so it was going to be steak and salad, followed by bought apple crumble and cream, with a bottle of good wine to elevate the menu.

The blue dress that he'd admired was going to have another airing, and if they weren't on better terms before the night was out she would be asking herself why.

She heard the fire-engine go past in the middle of the afternoon and wondered where they were off to, but once she became involved in feeding and bathing the baby and preparing the meal she forgot all about it.

Until there was a ring on the doorbell at just after six o'clock and she opened the door to find Geoff on the step.

'Alex has been hurt,' he said without preamble. 'He's in hospital with severe concussion and a head wound. If it hadn't been for his helmet he would have been killed. We were called out to a fire at the old print works and the roof fell in while we were dousing the flames.

'He was unconscious when we pulled him out but he came to in the ambulance for a few seconds and the first thing he said was for me to tell you what had happened.'

Geoff was observing her stricken face and he asked curiously, 'Were you expecting him here, or something?'

'Yes,' Zoey said in a daze as she tried to take in what he'd said. 'I'll go to him, Geoff. Which hospital is he in?'

'The General. Ward fifteen,' he informed her, still a bit nonplussed. 'Two of the guys will be going back to see him when they've had their meal but it will be later in the evening.'

'No problem,' she said hurriedly. 'I've got my little car.'

He nodded.

'Right, then. I'll be off. See you tomorrow, Zoey.'

When he'd gone she stood, frozen, in the hallway. She'd told Geoff that she was all right because she had her small car. That was the good news. What she'd forgotten for the briefest of moments was that she also had something else small in her possession. A sleeping baby!'

She would have to take Rosie with her. There was nothing else she could do. She had to get to Alex, to see for herself how badly hurt he was. Geoff would have played it down. They always did when one of them was injured.

When she got to the ward, breathless and dishevelled, a nurse stopped her and eyed the baby in her arms.

'Are you the firefighter's wife?' she questioned.

Zoey could see him lying quite still with his head heavily bandaged, and her heart missed a beat. She saw something else, too. He wasn't alone. Gloria was sitting beside the bed and on hearing the nurse's question she turned and said coolly, 'No, she isn't. I'm Mrs Carradine.'

The nurse's smile was apologetic as she turned to Zoey.

'I'm afraid that I'll have to ask you to leave, then. The patient is quite ill and only allowed one visitor.'

She stepped back in surprise when she found herself holding the baby and her eyes widened as Zoey walked purposefully towards the bed.

'I know. I won't be a second,' she told the nurse as the woman opened her mouth to protest. 'I have to see for myself how Alex is. Then I'll go.'

He looked pale and battered and would have no knowledge that she'd been. She planted a gentle kiss on top of the bandages and then held out her arms for the baby.

Gazing down on the sleeping Rosie, she told the nurse, 'The baby isn't his, you know. In case that's what you're thinking.' She pointed to a frowning Gloria. 'And neither is she!'

On that note she set off down the corridor, heels

clonking on the shining tiles and mind bogged down with worry and frustration.

The only comfort was that the first words Alex had said when he'd come round for those brief moments had been for her. She would have to hold onto that until there was more news from the hospital.

With Rosie once more in her cot, Zoey sat picking at the food she'd so zealously prepared. If she hadn't been so concerned about Alex she might have laughed at the spectacle of herself turning up at his bedside with the baby, like something out of a Victorian melodrama. And there'd been the expression on the nurse's face when she'd been putting her right about who was who.

But there wasn't a laugh in her at that moment. Supposing something even worse happened to Alex during the night and no one told her. She would go insane.

As if a higher presence was tuned into her anxieties, the two firefighters who'd gone to visit Alex called to see her at ten o'clock and they brought better news.

Gloria had been nowhere to be seen and they'd been allowed to sit by his bed.

'He came round while we were there,' one of them told her 'and although he was still groggy he sent you a message.' He grinned across at her. 'You must be well in there.'

'It's nothing like that,' she told them awkwardly. 'It's just that I'd invited him round for a meal.'

'Well, he says why haven't you been to see him? That he'd rather it had been your face that he saw when he woke up instead of ours, and we can't blame him for that.'

'I've been!' she exclaimed distractedly. 'And the

nurse wouldn't let me see him because Gloria was already there.'

'Go now, then,' he suggested. 'We'll stay to keep an eye on the baby.'

Zoey was on her feet.

'Would you? I'd be really grateful. I only hope I don't meet the same nurse as the one who turned me away.'

The ward was dimly lit when she got there and it was the night staff that she spoke to this time.

'I'm Alex's fiancé,' she fibbed. 'If I could just see him for a moment.'

'Go ahead,' a robust staff nurse told her, 'but don't be too long. He has a nasty head wound.'

Alex was lying with his eyes closed, but almost as if he sensed her presence he opened them the moment she reached his side.

'So you got my message,' he murmured drowsily.

'Yes, I did,' she said softly, taking his hand in hers.

'But you only came because I asked for you.'

'Of course not. Nothing would keep me away. I've been once but they wouldn't let me see you,' she said anxiously.

She waited for his response but there was none forthcoming.

'He's asleep again. Best not to disturb him,' the same nurse said from behind her.

Zoey got to her feet, thankful that he'd been aware of her presence if only for a few moments. How could he have doubted that she would come? she thought tearfully as she drove back home. Did he think she saw him only as someone to play around with?

If he'd been merely a colleague in her scheme of things she would still have gone to see him, but Alex held her heart in those big capable hands of his. Was he ever going to realise that?

The trouble was that Gloria had got in there first, sitting by his bed, staking her claim, as if he still belonged to her.

Zoey hoped that he wouldn't awaken in the morning still thinking she'd only visited him because he'd asked her to. He would have no idea of the state she'd been in ever since hearing about the accident.

Which was perhaps as well. He wouldn't have wanted the guys at the fire station to know that she was crazy about him, and if she wasn't careful that was exactly what they were going to think.

But none of that mattered as long as he made a full recovery. She'd had a quick glance at the chart at the bottom of his bed and seen that there were no skull fractures or suspected haematomas, so that was something to be thankful for. But the fact remained that he had a deep head wound and was far from being his normal self.

CHAPTER SIX

WHEN Alex awoke in the middle of the night the first thing he remembered was Zoey's face when she'd sat by the bed. She'd looked anxious and tearful and he wasn't sure why. Whether it was because she was worried about him, or because of something he'd said, he didn't know. Maybe a bit of both.

He knew he'd said something and although his thought processes were back to normal now, they hadn't been then. He'd felt muzzy and sleepy.

He wondered how she'd felt when he hadn't turned up for the meal. She was his prime concern. Everything about her mattered to him.

It wasn't that simple, though, was it? There was Gloria in the background. They had no future together. That was as sure as night following day, but he couldn't turn his back on her while she was so concerned about her aunt, which left Zoey to think that there were still feelings there.

Raising himself off the pillows, he looked around him. He could see all right and as he flexed himself under the sheets he decided that he could move all right, too. So when the new day appeared he would ask to be discharged.

If he'd known about Zoey's appearance like a rejected mistress by his bedside he might have managed a laugh, but as he didn't he remained in sombre mood. Until some hours later when the consultant came round and reluctantly agreed to discharge him.

'Any unpleasant after-effects or infection in the head wound, I want you back here immediately,' he said, 'and no reporting for duty until I've given you the all-clear.'

Zoey went to bed that night with what felt like a heavy weight inside her chest. When she looked at the bedside clock it seemed incredible that less than six hours ago she'd been planning the meal and been on the point of making herself beautiful for Alex.

And now he was hurt, in hospital, and under the impression that she wasn't all that bothered when in truth she'd visited him twice. Both times with little joy.

But the main thing was that he was alive and not as badly hurt as he might have been. She would go to see him again tomorrow and hope that it would be third time lucky.

It would have to be in the evening as she was on duty at the station all day, which could mean that Gloria or some of the men might be there. But she would have to chance that.

Yet it was a long time to wait for news of him, she thought the next morning and decided to go home at lunchtime to phone the hospital in privacy. She would feel better once she had a report on his progress.

As she walked up the cul-de-sac her step faltered. His car had just pulled up at the front of his house with Gloria in the driving seat. Sitting next to her was Alex, easily recognisable by the bulky bandage around his head.

'I don't believe it!' she said to no one in particular. 'He's home! It's too soon. What are they thinking of?'

He was easing himself out of the car when she reached

it, and as she stood observing him with amazed eyes he gave a quirky smile.

'Hi, Zoey. Surprised to see me?'

'Surprised? I'm appalled! You were comatose when I left you last night and earlier you'd been unconscious. They should have kept you for a few more days at least.'

'It was at my insistence,' he said. 'Don't fuss.'

'You are risking your physical well-being,' she persisted. Turning to Gloria who was gazing around her as if the discussion going on didn't concern her, she said, 'Why did you let Alex discharge himself?'

'It's not for me to tell him what to do,' she said with a shrug, and went on, adding to Zoey's outrage, 'Though you obviously think that you have the right.'

That made Zoey want to lash out.

'It's common sense we're talking about, not rights!'

She knew she was overreacting. Alex's expression told her that. Yet surely he realised that she was behaving like this because she loved him.

A feeling of anticlimax had swept over her when she'd seen him getting out of the car. After all her anxiety, here he was, home, and as cool as a cucumber.

'The doctor wouldn't have let me come home if he'd thought there was any risk,' he said with a restrained kind of patience that did nothing to calm her down.

He looked pale and tired and, immediately contrite, she said, 'I'm sorry. I'm keeping you out here when you should be inside, resting. I'll see you when you come back to work, Alex.' Then she said to Gloria with a steely glare, 'Look after him.' Off she went with outrage and misery vying for first place in her thoughts.

The need to phone the hospital had gone now that Alex was home so she went back to the station and told the others the news.

'Gee whiz!' Greg said. 'That's a quick recovery.'

Zoey turned away. So she wasn't the only one who thought it was a bit too soon for Alex to be out and about. 'Don't fuss,' he'd said. It was like him to play it down, but couldn't he see her point of view for once?

To deepen her gloom, Greg went on, 'So he doesn't want you over there, holding his hand, then? But I'm forgetting, he already has company, hasn't he?'

She glared at him.

'If you're trying to annoy me, you're succeeding. Don't push your luck, Osbourne.'

He laughed and reached for the top piece of toast on the pile that they always made for elevenses and she was left to her thoughts.

'What is the matter with that girl?' Gloria said irritably when they went inside the house. 'You haven't known her five minutes and she's acting as if she owns you.'

Alex gave her a long, level look.

'Don't pretend you're not aware that you're messing up my life, Gloria,' he said coolly. 'It isn't always the length of time one has known a person that counts. Look at you and I. We'd known each other for ever, but it didn't work out.

'Zoey is warm and caring with everyone she meets, and if she's prepared to pass some of it my way I consider myself lucky. But I've recently gone through the demoralising experience of divorce and if it's left you unscathed, it isn't like that for me. I don't want any more hurt for myself...or anyone else.'

'I don't want a lecture, Alexander,' she said huffily.

'All right, then. Just as long as we know where we stand. And regarding Zoey Lawrence...that's my business.'

In the privacy of his room he stood gazing bleakly through the window. Zoey had been horrified when she'd seen that he was home, but instead of taking her in his arms and telling her how much her concern meant to him, he'd told her to stop fussing.

Would they ever get it right? His head was aching. His usual clear thinking absent. If it hadn't been for the previous day's accident they might have reached a better understanding by now, but it was almost as if the Fates were conspiring to test them. Working in the background to complicate their lives.

He'd been looking forward to spending a quiet evening with Zoey. Had thought it might present an opportunity to tell her how he really felt about everything...the divorce, themselves, Gloria's continuing presence. But instead he'd ended up in hospital with his ex-wife on the front row and Zoey fretting on the sidelines.

If Zoey had known that Alex's day was taking its course just as dismally as her own, she might have felt better. But she had no way of knowing and as it dragged on with only one 'shout' to a chip-pan fire that mercifully the householder had dealt with sensibly before they'd got there, she felt her gloom deepen.

But a break was about to appear in the clouds. When she arrived home in the evening a radiant Mandy was waiting for her. She held out her hand and Zoey saw a diamond ring sparkling on her finger.

'What's this, then?' Zoey asked excitedly.

'Harry's asked me to marry him!' Mandy bubbled. 'We're engaged!'

'Fantastic!' Zoey crowed, her own woes forgotten. 'And what does Rosie have to say?'

'Gurgle, gurgle,' her delighted mother said laughingly, and Zoey joined in.

It was marvellous news. Mandy had found someone to love and cherish her, Zoey thought as they chatted excitedly about dates and wedding preparations.

Tonight wasn't the time to be thinking about her own future. Today was Mandy's. She would concern herself about her own affairs some other time.

If Alex and herself had been more in tune she would have wanted to dash across the road to tell him the good news. But did she want to have to impart it beneath Gloria's supercilious gaze? And would he think she had an underlying motive? Such as using it as a reminder that she would soon be free to pursue her own life?

No. That wasn't what she wanted. She would tell him when he was back on the job in more impersonal surroundings.

For the rest of the week Zoey made an effort to put Alex out of her mind. She caught occasional glimpses of him going in and out of the house, which seemed to indicate that he was no worse, and with that knowledge she forced herself to be content.

Mandy was planning a Christmas wedding. The day of Christmas Eve, to be exact, and once the first excitement had died down Zoey had told her, 'I'll move out before the wedding. You won't need me any more and you'll want the house to yourselves.'

As Mandy had opened her mouth to protest Zoey had forestalled her.

'It's true, Mandy. You don't want to start your life together with me around all the time. I'm truly happy for you. Harry is kind, generous and funny. You're a lucky woman…and I know Dad would have approved of what you're doing.'

'You are something else,' Mandy had said chokily. 'You gave up a lot to come here and now you must be wishing you'd stayed where you were.'

'Never!' she affirmed stoutly. 'For one thing, I've met the love of my life. It's taking him a while to get used to the idea, but I'm working on him.'

'We could have a double wedding,' the bride-to-be suggested, laughingly.

Zoey shook her head.

'No way. Alex and I seem to take one step forward and two steps back all the time. It doesn't made for easy communication with Gloria under his feet, but hopefully he'll soon be back on duty and we can make up for lost time.'

She was trying to sound positive, but deep down inside she wasn't quite so confident. It felt as if she was doing all the running. Yet there had been moments when it had seemed as if paradise beckoned. When she'd known beyond doubt that Alex cared. But they'd been few and far between.

There was much more happening in Mandy's life at the moment and Zoey wasn't feeling as calm about finding somewhere else to live as she made out.

She didn't know whether it was going to be easy or not. It would have to be close to the fire station for one thing. Was it time to consider buying a property of her own, or would rental be more in keeping with the uncertainty of her present existence?

With that thought in mind she went into the local estate agent's during her lunch hour to check on the prices and availability of suitable flats or small houses.

As she was leaving she came face to face with Alex.

His glance went immediately to the brochures in her hand, while Zoey's wide gaze was taking in the fact that the bandages had gone, to be replaced by a large sterile dressing.

It was their first meeting since the day he'd been discharged from hospital and it seemed like a lifetime. For some reason she felt tongue-tied and off balance and it was he who spoke first.

'What's with the brochures, Zoey? Not thinking of moving, are you?'

She was beginning to gather her wits and told him breezily, ''Fraid so. Mandy's throwing me out.'

He smiled but it didn't reach his eyes.

'You don't expect me to believe that.'

'You might. One never knows. But, no, the truth of the matter is that she's getting married…on Christmas Eve…and Rosie and I are going to be bridesmaids. Isn't that marvelous?'

'To the guy from the pizza place?'

'Yes, to Harry.'

He was sombre now.

'And so where does that leave you? Amongst the nation's homeless?'

'Not really, but I am looking for a place of my own. Mandy and Harry will need space—it's my choice to move out.'

'It seems a bit unfair that you've uprooted yourself to come here and then find out it was all for nothing.'

Her face had clouded.

'It wasn't for nothing, Alex. My being here gave Mandy the chance to do some socialising. Otherwise she might never have met Harry.'

And I wouldn't have met you, she wanted to tell him, but it was the kind of thing best said when she was in his arms, if that ever happened again, not eyeing him achingly on the main street.

'Your head, how is it?' she asked, changing the subject.

'Fine. I'll be back on the job after the weekend and for various reasons I can't wait.'

That makes two of us, she thought wistfully.

'I've been to see Geoff's son while I've been attending the hospital,' he was saying. 'Has he told you that the lad is being discharged next week?'

'Yes. He's done well to make such a quick recovery under the circumstances, hasn't he?'

Alex nodded.

'He was a crazy young fool, tampering with stuff in the lab, and sadly has paid the price. But as is often the case with that age group, he's bounced back remarkably well. He'll have to keep going back for skin grafts, of course.'

She sighed. What would they be discussing next? The weather? Anything but themselves.

'I have to go, Alex,' she told him abruptly. 'Or they'll be sending out a search party for me.'

He took a step back and she knew he'd got the message. Now it was his turn to sound regretful as he said, 'Yes, of course. Blame me if the guys want to know where you've been.'

As they went their separate ways Alex was fuming for various reasons. Why hadn't he told Zoey how much he was missing her? Told her she could stay at his place if she hadn't found anywhere to live in time? Even though he knew that her young stepmother would never leave her out in the cold.

The two women were close. They had a loving relationship and Zoey, kind and unselfish, would never blame Mandy for letting her move out here, only to find herself surplus to requirements.

Yet he wasn't happy about the set-up. In fact, he wasn't happy about anything at the moment. When he'd met Zoey outside the estate agent's he'd had to take a grip on himself. He'd wanted to reach out for her, take her in his arms and tell her how he ached to be with her. How he was sorry for the way he'd been the last time they'd met and…

But she'd taken the wind out of his sails by telling him about her change in circumstances and now he was putting his own longings to one side in concern for her.

Alex sighed. It was crazy to think of offering Zoey accommodation at his place…with Gloria around. His gloom deepened as another depressing thought reared its head. Would Zoey see this recent turn of events as a reason to go back to the city? To the area's biggest fire station where she'd been based before? He sincerely hoped not.

The eating place belonging to the Harry fellow was just across the way. Maybe he would have a pizza for his lunch and at the same time ask a few searching questions of the man whose life was taking an upward turn, unlike his own.

He didn't have to introduce himself. As he ordered the food the pleasant man behind the counter said, 'You're the officer in charge at the fire station, aren't you? The guy who lives across from Mandy and Zoey?'

Alex smiled.

'Yes, that's me…and…er…it's because Zoey's a member of my team that I've come in to have a word with you.'

So much for subtlety, he thought wryly, but he was in no mood for beating about the bush.

'Go ahead,' the other man said.

'I'm concerned that she may end up with nowhere to live after moving out here to be with Mandy and the baby.'

Harry was looking worried.

'Zoey doesn't have to move out on my account. She was there before I came on the scene and I'd be happy for her to stay. It was her own idea to go. I think she wants to give us some space, but I feel the same as you, that she mustn't be left in a position where she has nowhere to live. If I'd had a house of my own we could have gone there, but there's only a poky flat up above this place and, although it suffices for me, it would be no fit place for a baby.'

'I agree,' Alex told him, 'and I must say I feel happier knowing that you have Zoey's best interests at heart.'

'Just how far does your concern for her extend?' Harry asked quizzically. 'According to what I've heard, Zoey cares for you a lot. Mandy and I thought a double wedding might be on the cards.'

Alex felt his jaw slacken.

'Wha-at?'

'Hmm. It's true.'

'And what did Zoey say to that?'

'Put the dampener on it straight away, from all accounts. Seemed to think you were too engrossed in your ex-wife.'

'And if that turned out not to be true...what then?'

Harry laughed.

'I've no idea. You'll have to ask her yourself.'

'I might just do that,' Alex told him purposefully, and once he'd finished eating he pointed himself in the direction of home. What he had to say to Zoey would have to wait until the evening. He'd no wish to have a discussion with her while all the men were listening in. But once she'd had time to eat her evening meal he would go across and talk to her.

'Alex!' Zoey exclaimed when she saw him on the doorstep. 'This is too much! The pleasure of your company twice in one day.'

'You'll be having that same pleasure all day and every day from next Monday onwards,' he said with a glint in his eye. 'Just look upon today as a breaking in. I want to talk to you, Zoey. Is it convenient?'

She inclined her head graciously and stepped back. As he strode over the threshold he said, 'Are you alone?'

'Yes. Why? Have you come to seduce me?'

He laughed.

'You're very saucy tonight.'

'Aren't I just.'

It was a cover-up, of course. In truth, she was nervous and on edge. What did he want to talk about? As far as she was concerned, nothing had changed since their meeting earlier in the day, but Alex had a look of purpose about him.

She was as beautiful and bouncy as ever, he thought, but she looked tired. There were dark smudges beneath her incredible eyes and she'd lost weight. He hoped he wasn't to blame for either of those things, yet he had a feeling that he might be.

'I want to talk to you about Gloria,' he said gravely.

He watched Zoey stiffen and thought that had been a bad opening.

'I thought you might be here because of us,' she said flatly. 'What about her?'

'I just want you to know that there is nothing between us any more. I know that she was in the forefront when

I was in hospital, but as I was in no fit state to argue I wasn't able to do anything about it.

'I also know that you were hurt and angry because you weren't involved and because I appeared to treat your anxieties too lightly. I certainly didn't mean it to seem like that, Zoey. If I was insensitive, I'm sorry. Maybe I'm out of touch with tender loving care, but I do recognize it when I see it. So will you forgive me?'

She was about to tell him that of course she would when he amazed her by saying lightly, 'I can't promise a double wedding, though.'

Zoey could feel her cheeks starting to burn. How had he found out about Mandy's teasing? As if he'd read her mind, Alex went on, 'Harry told me. I was in his place at lunchtime.'

'It was just a joke,' she gabbled weakly, 'on Mandy's part. It wasn't me rushing in where angels fear to tread. I wasn't presuming anything.'

'No, of course not,' he agreed smoothly, adding to her discomfort.

She'd been delighted to see him, but now she just wanted him to go while she got over her embarrassment, but Alex had other ideas.

'So you do understand that Gloria and I are finished for all time? The only woman I'm interested in is you, and if you would just let me get my breath I might get around to doing something about it.'

Her face had softened.

'Is that a promise?'

'Come here and I'll show you.'

His kisses were gentle and passionless this time. As if he knew she'd been hurting and wanted to take away the pain first. And as she nestled against him Zoey thought, It's going to come right. I can tell.

'We've got a lot of catching up to do,' he murmured against the bright cap of her hair.

She laughed up at him, her embarrassment forgotten.

'I've no objections to that.' As if an imp of mischief was on her shoulder, she added, 'What else did Harry say about me?'

Alex was smiling.

'Oh, that you fancied me like mad and that he wouldn't dream of turning you out onto the streets.'

He was joking, but saw from her expression that she wasn't amused.

'So you think it's funny, discussing my innermost feelings with Harry...and the pair of you talking over where I'm going to live. I'm not exactly an idiot, you know, Alex. I can sort out my own affairs. I'd like to see your face if I told someone about your feelings...and made it known what was going on in your establishment.'

He groaned.

'Here we go again! Me saying the wrong thing and you taking umbrage. You're making a fuss about nothing. Why do you think I went in there?'

'Not to have a pizza, from the sound of it.'

'Correct. If you'll calm down, I'll explain.'

'Don't patronise me!' she hissed.

'I'm not!' he told her, his voice hardening. 'You're as prickly as a hedgehog.'

'Yes, well, they're always getting flattened, too. I think you'd better go,' she said wearily, as her annoyance drained away.

'No!' he said firmly. 'Not until I've imparted a few home truths. You say I'm the love of your life. Well, how about considering my feelings for a change? Do you think I like the idea of being roped in as part of a double wedding without it even being mentioned? It would seem that you're not the only one who gets discussed behind their back.'

'Nobody has roped you into anything,' Zoey protested.

This time he was prepared to go. The tender moments they'd been sharing had turned sour because of an innocent conversation with Harry. He'd gone there because he'd been concerned about Zoey. Because he felt she was getting a raw deal. But it would seem that he'd touched on a sore spot as far as she was concerned.

With his hand on the doorhandle he said, 'This is totally ridiculous, rowing like this. I came over with the very best of intentions and look where it's got me. I'll see you on Monday at the fire station. Maybe by then we'll both be feeling calmer.'

In the process of deflating like a pricked balloon, she turned away. 'Yes, maybe we will, Alex. By then I might be seeing everything more clearly.'

He could have questioned what she'd meant by that, but he felt there'd already been enough lack of communication. No point in risking more, so he went.

During the weekend Zoey viewed a couple of flats and a small cottage, all within a short distance of the fire station. Her interest was lukewarm. Finding somewhere to live was going to be a necessity, but she couldn't work up any enthusiasm after the quarrel with Alex.

She kept telling herself she'd been unreasonable. That she'd flipped because he'd found out about the double marriage suggestion. But there'd also been pique in her because she was being seen as unable to look after herself.

It was a nuisance that she was going to have to find

somewhere else to live. But she was so happy for Mandy that it was a small price to pay, and once she started looking in earnest it shouldn't be a problem. She would find somewhere. There was no reason for Alex and Harry to get involved.

Harry called round on the Sunday night and asked with a twinkle in his eye, 'Have you had a visit from your firefighter friend? When I talked to him earlier in the week I got the impression that he might be going to pop the question.'

Her throat had gone dry. Pop what question? Harry couldn't be serious.

'He's been round, yes,' she told him, 'but it was only to tell me that he has completely finished with his ex-wife. He didn't pop any question.'

Doubts were choking her. She hadn't given him the chance, had she? The moment Alex had opened his mouth she'd jumped down his throat.

'So he's not in favour of the double wedding idea?' Harry persisted.

'It would seem not,' she said tonelessly. 'He was just as annoyed as I was at being discussed by a third party.'

Harry's face clouded.

'Gee, I'm sorry, Zoey. It wasn't meant to be gossip. That bit just slipped out, more as a joke than anything. He came to see me because he was so concerned about you. Worried in case you were going to end up with nowhere to live.'

'Oh, no!' she exclaimed. 'Alex did that? And all he got from me was a tirade of pettish abuse!'

How was she going to face him in the morning?

With that thought still uppermost in her mind, Zoey was in sombre mood as she prepared to leave for work the next morning, but as she opened the door to a blast of cold air Mandy came into the hallway with Rosie in her arms.

'It's through, Zoey!' she crowed. 'The young miss has got her first tooth.'

'Oh, that's lovely,' she said, looking down at her young stepsister's smooth face. There was a bright spot of colour on each of the baby's cheeks. That, along with uncharacteristic fretfulness, had told them that teeth were on the way, and now the first one was through.

And so as Zoey stepped out into the December morning there was a smile on her face and a new lightness in her step. To the man who was about to leave his own home for the same destination it was an indication that the girl of his dreams wasn't feeling anywhere near as despondent as he was.

Maybe it was better to leave things as they were, he thought. If Zoey wasn't bothered about their quarrel, what was the point of trying to put things right?

They arrived simultaneously and it seemed to her that this was the moment to say she was sorry, while they were outside on the fire-station forecourt.

'Good morning,' Alex said coolly. 'I saw you leaving the house looking very happy.'

'Happy?' she echoed blankly, as she tried to control the bone-melting feeling that was always there when she saw him after even the shortest of absences. 'Oh, yes, of course. Rosie cut her first tooth this morning. Just what I needed to cheer me up.'

'Why? Did you feel that you needed cheering up?'

'What do you think, Alex? I spoke to Harry last night and he explained why you'd been to see him. I'm totally contrite and in future will keep my mouth zipped.'

He was laughing as relief coursed through him. So

she had been just as upset as he'd been. Thank goodness for that.

She was bouncing back.

'So we can start catching up on that lost time whenever you like.'

His amusement increased.

'I'll bear that in mind, as I take it that you're not meaning for me to commence at this exact moment.'

Zoey looked around her. Dorothea was attacking the entrance to the fire station with mop and bucket. Greg and one of the other firemen had just driven onto the forecourt. She pretended to consider.

'Er…no. Later maybe. How about the park at lunchtime?'

'Bit fresh for sitting on wooden benches, isn't it?'

Her eyes were sparkling.

'We'll have our love to keep us warm,' she said, adding with unconscious wistfulness, 'Won't we?'

'You are something else, Zoey Lawrence,' he told her in a low voice. 'Will you please stop looking at me like that? Or I'll start now, whether we have an audience or not.'

CHAPTER SEVEN

IT WAS cold in the park. A chill wind nipped Zoey's ankles and lifted what were left of autumn's dry leaves, but she was barely aware of the fact.

Apart from a woman walking a snappy little dog and an old man shuffling along, she and Alex were the only ones there. For a short space of time they were alone, and the trysting place didn't matter as long as Alex was strolling beside her and holding her hand.

She'd thought a couple of times during the morning that they wouldn't be able to get away. The crew had no sooner reported for duty than they'd been called out to a house fire on a nearby council estate where children had been trapped in an upstairs bedroom.

They'd arrived to find the mother screaming hysterically in the back garden and the demented father being held back by neighbours.

'Our two boys are in the bedroom,' the man had cried as the fire-engine had screeched to a halt. Breaking free, he'd ran towards the open back door.

Alex had flung himself off the engine and grabbed him by the arms. 'This is our job. We'll tackle this. Stay back, sir.'

They'd brought them out through the bedroom window. Alex and Greg had gone in and found the children huddled behind one of the beds. As they'd brought them down the ladder to safety a cheer had gone up from the anxious onlookers, and while the rest of the crew had concentrated on putting out the blaze, Zoey had concentrated on the children.

The small boys were both in shock and suffering from some degree of smoke inhalation. They also had minor burns to the upper arms and legs but thankfully they were alive. The elder of the two had prevented it from being much worse by having the presence of mind to slam shut the bedroom door when he'd seen the flames coming from an airing cupboard and engulfing the landing and stairs.

It seemed that the parents, who had just got up, had smelt smoke coming from upstairs while they'd been preparing breakfast. The father had traced its source to the landing and when he'd opened the cupboard door flames had leapt out to such an extent that he hadn't been able to get past them to the bedroom where the children had been getting dressed.

Faulty wiring had been the cause, as it so often was in those sorts of incidents. Once the blaze was under control they went into the premises and inspected what was left of the upstairs electrical wiring. The quality and arrangement of the wires had told its own tale.

She gave the children oxygen, covered the burns with temporary dressings and asked a neighbour to provide some hot sweet tea to counteract shock for both parents and children.

By the time the crew got back to the station the morning was well under way but its events weren't over.

Jeremy, the lad who'd been trapped in the car on the hill bend all those weeks ago, appeared and, after receiving a warm welcome, was shown around the station.

He looked gaunt and, although off crutches, still needed a stick to lean on, but there was nothing frail about his determination to join the force.

'As soon as I'm really fit I'm going to apply,' he told
them. 'You guys were the most welcome sight I'd ever
seen when I looked up from that mangled mess I was
trapped in.'

'You'll have to concentrate on getting back to full
health and strength,' Alex told him. 'The fitness tests
you have to undergo to join the fire service are very
stringent.'

'What's the routine?' the would-be firefighter asked.

'Basic training takes two years. The first fourteen
weeks are spent on a residential course at the Brigade
Training Building in the city centre and it covers a lot
of things.'

'Such as?'

'Handling equipment, first aid, chemistry, physics, hy-
draulics, building construction, general fire safety…'

'No problem. I'll do it,' the lad told him with the
sublime confidence of youth, and for some reason none
of them had doubted that he would.

At last a late lunch-break arrived and they were off,
separately at first, joining up by the park gates.

'So tell me about the wedding,' Alex said as they
walked towards an ornamental lake of cold grey water
which was being whipped up by the wind. 'That is, if
the subject isn't taboo.'

Zoey smiled up at him.

'Of course it isn't. I wasn't the one who was making
a fuss about Mandy's suggestion. Like I said, she was
joking.'

He rolled his eyes heavenwards.

'All right. I get the message. So what about the wedding?'

'Mandy is going to wear a long cream brocade dress
which will go beautifully with her brown hair and eyes.

Rosie and I are going to be dressed in blue velvet
trimmed with white fur—fake, of course.'

'Unless that little one qualifies for the *Guinness Book
of Records* as a child who walked at five months, I don't
see how she's going to be a bridesmaid at her mother's
wedding.'

'I'm going to carry her, of course.'

'I see.'

He would have liked to have told her that it would be
totally enchanting to have seen the two of them together,
but he had no intention of putting a foot wrong today.
He wanted a relationship with Zoey and he fully intended to pursue it, but in his own time. There was still
the thought of Gloria hanging over his head like the
sword of Damocles.

'I shall come to watch.'

'You might find yourself doing more than that.'

'What do you mean?'

'Mandy wants to know if you'll give her away as she
has no male relatives.'

There was surprise in Alex's dark gaze.

'Really? Well…yes…I suppose so. I will if she wants
me to.'

'She does…and so do I.'

'Tell me the arrangements, then.'

'The ceremony is at half past three at St James's
Church on Monday the twenty-fourth of December, followed by a meal. There will be just the five of us.
Mandy, Harry, Rosie, and you and I. Afterwards the bridal couple are going away for a few days.'

'And taking the baby with them?'

'Er…no. I'm taking a week's leave to look after
Rosie.'

He was frowning.

'What sort of a Christmas is that going to be for you?'

Zoey had stopped and was looking up at him.

'We could pretend she's ours and play happy families.'

Alex touched her cold cheek gently but didn't take her up on the suggestion.

'So you won't be moving out of Mandy's house until they come back from their honeymoon?'

'Mmm, that's right. Why do you ask?'

'No special reason. I'm just curious.'

Of course, there was a reason, but it didn't seem like the moment to tell her that he hoped to have sorted out his affairs by then and might have some ideas of his own about where she was going to live.

There was peace between them and he didn't want to spoil it, so he changed the subject to one less delicate.

'I'm applying for the Station Officer vacancy,' he told her. 'As I'm virtually doing the job already, it seems logical to seek the proper status. During the coming weeks I'll be taking written and practical examinations and appearing before the selection panel at Command Headquarters.'

Zoey smiled up at him.

'I really will have to behave myself then, won't I? Will I have to call you "sir"?'

'Yes, and bend the knee,' he teased. 'Seriously, the only difference will be that I'll be wearing a white helmet instead of a yellow one.'

It wasn't strictly true. There would be more responsibility with the promotion but the time to concern himself about that was when he got the job.

He checked his watch.

'We're going to have to make tracks, Zoey. The

lunch-break is almost up. Have you enjoyed our stroll in these sub-zero temperatures?'

She pretended to shiver but her glowing cheeks belied the pretence.

'Yes, I have,' she told him, 'but we do have the means to generate some heat of our own, you know. Melt frost with fire.'

He bent his mouth to hers.

'What a good idea.'

'Mmm,' she murmured as his arms went around her, and it was like the other night. Only this time she wasn't going to spoil it. A warm tide of longing was running through her veins.

She could have stayed there for ever in the deserted park. But there was nothing to guarantee that the cold weather meant there would be no fires to attend or accidents on icy roads. As they drew apart, she said softly, 'We'd better go before we're missed.'

Alex nodded.

'Yes. There'll be other times. If we'll let it, life can only get better for us.'

The afternoon was uneventful and as the fire crew left the station in the early evening, after switching the call-out system through to headquarters, Alex caught up with her.

'What have you planned for tonight?' he asked casually.

'Er...nothing really. The lady who's making our dresses for the wedding is coming round for a fitting session but that shouldn't take long. What did you have in mind?'

He smiled, and Zoey saw contentment in his gaze.

'Nothing in particular. Certainly not another sojourn

in the arctic waste that the park has turned into. Maybe
we could have a bite somewhere and a nice long chat.'

He saw her expression and his smile wavered.

'Is that not exciting enough for you?'

She looked away, not meeting his glance.

'That would be great. I was only thinking that privacy
is a hard thing to come by in our two lives.'

'You mean with Gloria at my place and Mandy and
the baby at your end?'

'Yes.'

He didn't take her up on that. The subject of Gloria
was like walking on stony ground.

Instead, he said, 'I'll pick you up in an hour if that's
all right with you. And, Zoey...'

'Yes?' she breathed.

'Wrap up warmly. There's going to be a keen frost
tonight.'

'Is that all?'

She could see his eyes glinting beneath the streetlamps.

'For the moment...yes.'

'Which, interpreted, means don't rush you.'

'Yes, something like that.'

He gave her a gentle push.

'Go on in. Mandy will be thinking you've got lost.'

It seemed that Gloria had been watching them from the
window. The moment Alex turned his key in the lock
she was there, and he wondered in sudden irritation why
she didn't get a life of her own. Unable to help himself,
he referred to it in an oblique sort of way.

'How's your aunt?'

'A bit better,' was the abrupt reply, and he sensed that
something had ruffled her feathers.

'When is she going to be transferred back to the rest home?'

'Soon, I hope.'

'Your clients must be wondering what's happened to you.'

'Possibly.'

Alex observed her thoughtfully.

'What's wrong, Gloria? Who's upset you?'

She answered the question with another one.

'Are you in love with Zoey Lawrence?'

He smiled. For the first time he was ready to admit it.

'Yes.'

'I see.'

'Good,' he remarked blandly. 'That's all right, then.' When she had nothing further to say he went up to his room to change.

As he came down the stairs she was taking a phone call and he heard her say. 'Right. We'll come straight away.' Then she began to weep.

'Who was that?' he asked quickly.

'The cottage hospital,' she sobbed. 'Aunt Mary's had a stroke. You'll have to take me, Alex. I'm too upset to drive.'

'Yes, of course,' he agreed, and knew that he wasn't going to be able to keep to the arrangements he'd made with Zoey.

When the phone rang Zoey was almost ready, snugly attired in a soft blue angora jumper, trousers and a three-quarter-length black coat with a neat fun-fur collar.

Her eyes were sparkling at the thought of the evening ahead, but the sparkle faded when she heard what he had to say.

'Yes, of course I understand that you have to take her,' she said tonelessly. 'I hope Gloria's aunt isn't too badly affected.'

Alex sighed. He knew Zoey was disappointed. So was he, but he could hardly leave Gloria at such a time. He owed it to her, if only for old times' sake.

'I'll be in touch as soon as I get back,' he promised, 'but we could be there for hours if it's as serious as Gloria seems to think.'

'Yes. I realise that,' Zoey told him. 'You'd better go—we'll see each other soon.'

'What a shame that your evening has been spoilt,' Mandy said when she heard what had happened. 'You look lovely. It's a shame to waste it. Why don't you go to the pub? If Alex can't be there the rest of them will be, and from what you say they're always pleased to see you.'

Zoey hesitated. She knew that Harry was coming round and that he and Mandy would be happy to have the place to themselves for a while. But going to the pub would be a poor replacement for a quiet evening with Alex.

'All right,' she agreed. 'You've persuaded me. If Alex gets back earlier than expected, you can tell him where to find me.'

Greg was at her side within seconds when Zoey arrived at The Wheatsheaf and for the rest of the evening he monopolised her.

Miserable that he was available when Alex wasn't, she didn't object. She'd no illusions about the man. He was a womaniser, conceited and always had an eye to the main chance. He was also getting very drunk. But at least he was someone to talk to as the minutes ticked by and there was no sign of Alex.

When it was time to go home she made no comment when he fell into step beside her, as they both lived in the same direction. When he drunkenly draped his arm around her shoulders as they strolled along beneath a moonlit sky she didn't make a fuss because she was so preoccupied with her own thoughts. She also thought he might fall over without some support.

They were at her gate and the look in his eyes told her that he wasn't in a hurry to get home to his bachelor pad. She reached out for the latch but he pulled her back.

'What's the hurry?' he slurred. 'Don't you want some company now that action man's not here?'

The house was in darkness so it looked as if Harry had gone.

'I don't think so,' she told him firmly, shrugging off the arm that was tightening around her shoulders. 'I'm tired. It's been a long day. And, Greg…'

'What?' he asked, bringing his face close to hers.

'The fact that we chatted in the pub doesn't mean that it's payback time. In fact, it won't ever be that. Do you understand?'

But Greg had had so much to drink, he wasn't listening. Suddenly he grabbed her in a bear hug and kissed her on the lips. Frantically, Zoey tried to avoid his mouth and struggle free from his grip, but it was almost impossible.

Then, as if by magic, Alex was there on the pavement with them, dragging Greg away from her, almost lifting him off his feet in his fury, and she was staggering back against the gate with her hand against her mouth and her legs wilting beneath her.

'Clear off!' Alex told him. 'If you lay a finger on Zoey again you'll have me to deal with.'

Greg had got the message and was backing off, but he wasn't quite finished.

'Ask her who she's been making eyes at all the time we've been in the pub,' he muttered, and with that he went staggering off.

'Thanks for that, Alex,' Zoey said tearfully. 'I should have seen it coming.'

His face was like granite and the words when they came were just as cold.

'Don't apologise. I don't own you…and if I'd thought I did, that little episode would have made me see differently. The next time you feel inclined to tell me how much you care for me, throw in an explanation as to why the moment my back was turned you sought Osbourne out.'

Her hand was still over her mouth, as if she didn't want Alex to see the lips that another man had kissed. Observing it, he said coldly, 'If you have a thick lip in the morning, I'll know why, won't I?'

She opened her mouth to tell him that she was sorry. That she'd only chatted to Greg because she'd been miserable and at a loose end, but he didn't give her the chance. He'd turned on his heel and was striding back to where he'd come from with the set of his shoulders telling their own story.

As she walked wearily up the garden path, Zoey wondered how long he'd been back and how the old lady was, as she hadn't been given the chance to ask.

When Alex went back inside his house he was relieved that Gloria was asleep in the spare room and not around to witness his dejection.

They'd found her aunt unconscious after the stroke and had been told that she wasn't expected to recover. At eleven o'clock they'd left her bedside with a promise from the nursing staff that they would ring if there was any change.

When he'd got home he'd seen that the house across the way had been in darkness and had resigned himself to having to wait until morning before he spoke to Zoey.

He knew that she was impatient for progress in their relationship and all the time was being thwarted by the situation at his end. Tonight had been yet another frustrating postponement of getting to know each other better.

All of that he understood, but to kill time with Osbourne in his absence and let him come on to her like that was trying his own reserves to the limit.

He'd been gazing sombrely across at Mandy's house when he'd seen them walking up the cul-de-sac. Greg's arm had been around her and Zoey hadn't been complaining.

Raw anger had ripped through him to discover that she'd substituted the station Romeo for himself so quickly. Then it had become concern when he'd seen her fighting Osbourne off. So how did he feel right now? That he'd been right to be wary of getting involved in another relationship so soon?

For the rest of that week Greg avoided Zoey and Alex treated her with such glacial indifference that she clung to the breezy, cheerful normality of the rest of the fire crew like a soul in torment, which was what she was.

It wasn't in her nature to be deceitful or immoral, and if she'd expected an escapist night at the pub to turn out like it had she would have stayed in. But the damage

had been done. Alex had put her outside the circle of
his life and from the looks of it that was where she was
going to stay.

But she kept telling herself there was light in the darkness. It was only two weeks to the wedding. He'd agreed
to give Mandy away and, even if her own behaviour was
unreliable, his wasn't.

Maybe on that occasion they might find a level of
understanding that would take away the salt of the tears
that she kept shedding. The wedding was the only thing
she had to look forward to, as Christmas with just Rosie
for company looked like being a non-event.

'I'm going across to have a word with Alex about the
wedding,' Mandy said one evening. 'I don't suppose you
want to come?'

She knew they'd fallen out, but didn't seem unduly
bothered. Probably because Zoey had played down the
quarrel, leaving Mandy confident that he would be available to give her away.

Zoey sighed.

'No, thanks. I'm not his favorite person at the moment. I'll bath Rosie while you're gone, if you like.'

As her tiny stepsister gurgled in the bath water, Zoey
looked down at her wistfully.

'Why is it that your mummy's romance is so happy
and uncomplicated, little rosebud,' she said, 'while mine
is like a disaster area? Am I being too defeatist 'cos I'm
sick of eating humble pie? But neither can I face a large
helping of rebuff.'

She reached for a large white towel and, lifting the
baby carefully out of the water, began to pat her dry. As
she did so, her mind went back to what she'd said to
Alex about the three of them playing happy families.

When she'd said it she'd been thinking that one day

they might have a family of their own. She must have been crazy.

'That ex-wife of his is a pain,' Mandy said when she came back. 'She behaves as if they've never been divorced. She's dug in there, Zoey, and from the looks of it has no intentions of moving, even though her elderly aunt has passed away.'

'Has she? Oh, dear!' Zoey exclaimed. 'That's awful, but maybe Gloria will go now. When did it happen?'

'Early this evening. They'd just got back from the hospital when I got there.'

'So you didn't get the chance to discuss the wedding.'

'Alex and I had a quick word. No problem there. He's going to do the honours.'

'Thank goodness for that!' Zoey breathed. With the wistfulness still upon her, she said, 'Did he mention me?'

'Er…no.'

'Ugh,' she moaned. 'What am I going to do, Mandy? I really do love him.'

'Take each day as it comes,' she advised. 'Alex will come round. You just have to give him time.'

Zoey was taking each day as it came and none of them were bringing much joy. But whatever doldrums the man in charge and the latest member of the team might be wallowing in, the rest of the firefighters made up for it in light-hearted anticipation of the fast-approaching festive season.

One of the men had turned up with a tree. Another had brought decorations to be hung from the ceiling of the station and, in spite of her gloom, Zoey couldn't resist joining in.

She was on top of a step ladder when a 'shout' came

through, and as the men dropped what they were doing and hurried to climb aboard the fire-engine one of them caught the bottom of the ladder and it began to topple.

As it rocked she lost her balance and would have fallen if someone hadn't been there to break her descent.

'For goodness' sake, watch what you're doing,' Alex said as she looked up at him from the circle of his arms. 'You are totally careless.'

'I'm not!' she protested.

'Yes, you are,' he insisted, 'in more ways than one.'

'You're referring to the people I mix with, I suppose,' she breathed as they grabbed their fireproof jackets.

'Possibly.'

'You're an unforgiving soul,' she flared in sudden anger. 'I didn't know that Greg was going to jump on me. He was drunk. All I'd done was chat to him in the pub. Surely there was no crime in that.'

'So you don't see anything wrong in leading someone on without considering the consequences.'

'You can believe what you like,' she snapped as they took their places on the engine. 'But I didn't lead him on. I wish you weren't coming to the wedding.'

There was irony in his smile.

'Well, hard lines. I've promised Mandy, who, I must say, is a far less complicated person than you, that I will give her away and I intend to do just that.'

The blaze they'd been called out to, an area of dry scrubland that had been accidentally set alight, appeared on the skyline and it was time to put aside personal differences. But it didn't stop Zoey from bringing into the light of day a half-formed decision that had been at the back of her mind ever since the aftermath of the Greg Osbourne episode.

She and Alex were going nowhere. She was going to

ask to be transferred back to where she'd come from. There were plenty of flats in the city. It would solve the problem of somewhere to live once Mandy was married, and she could start to pick up the pieces after a disastrous romance. Any further than that she didn't want to think.

'You'll be able to join in the Christmas promotion down on the main street of our community this year,' Mandy said one morning as they breakfasted together.

Zoey observed her doubtfully.

'What do you mean?'

'We all try to do our bit to bring business to the traders on the cobbled street down by the river. There will be a big Christmas tree in the square, and smaller illuminated ones above every shop. At midday one of the local officials turns on the lights and then the fun starts.

'All the shopkeepers are dressed in old-fashioned clothes and they serve those who go into their premises with hot mince pies and mulled wine. There'll be Morris dancers, a carousel for the children, a popcorn stall, various outdoor craft presentations and a brass band, amongst other things.'

'Really!' Zoey exclaimed. 'What a good idea. When is it?'

'Next Saturday.'

'Right. So are we going to be there?'

Mandy smiled.

'I am, certainly. I'll be supporting Harry in his place.'

'Dressed up?'

'Yes, I suppose so…and with regard to yourself, the folk at the post office and general store want to know if you'll help out as they're going to be short-staffed on that day.'

'And what would I be wearing?'

'Oh, you know.'

Zoey laughed. 'No, I don't.'

'A long dress, an apron and a mob-cap.'

She groaned. 'Oh, dear! Not very captivating.'

It was Mandy's turn to laugh. 'I think you'll look lovely in that garb. So, what do you say? Shall I tell them that you'll oblige?'

Zoey sighed. 'Yes. I suppose so. I've nothing else to occupy my time with.'

'So you're still on the outside where Alex is concerned?'

'Mmm. Well and truly.'

'Maybe he'll relent when he sees another side to you,' Mandy teased.

'What? Looking like a character out of Charles Dickens? And who's the bigwig who'll be turning on the lights?'

'It's not a bigwig. Just someone of local prominence. This year they're honouring your lot.'

Zoey's eyes had widened.

'The fire service?'

'Yes.'

'It's not Alex, is it?'

'The same. Our popular fire chief. So, you see, we're all involved.'

'No one's mentioned it at the station.'

'He probably doesn't want a big thing made of it.'

Zoey found herself perking up. Maybe he would come in for a glass of wine or a mince pie, and if he didn't she would go to seek him out, even though the chill would probably still be persisting. At least she would be in his vicinity for part of that weekend.

*   *   *

It was a cold, clear morning, and by midday, when the festivities were due to start, a pale sun was warming the cobblestone street. There was already a festive atmosphere all around, and as Zoey observed herself in the big mirror at the back of the shop she was smiling for two reasons.

Firstly, because she was looking forward to the afternoon ahead and, secondly, because she was almost unrecognisable in the clothes that they'd found for her. With the mob-cap pulled well down over her golden bob, she wouldn't stand out in the crowd when Alex turned on the lights. Not that she was expecting him to be interested if she did.

It was one o'clock. The moment had arrived and when they all went to gather in the square for the 'turn-on' she was filled with pleasurable expectancy...until she saw Gloria beside Alex. It was a week since her aunt's funeral and she was still around. It looked as if Mandy had been right. She was dug in at Alex's place.

Zoey turned away. The day had lost its appeal. Alex's ex-wife was standing beside him looking elegant and relaxed, while she herself was dressed in somebody's grandmother's cast-off clothes.

He was making a short speech, but it was washing over her. Then he was reaching out for the switch and a cheer went up as the lights came on.

Yet in spite of the afternoon's depressing beginning, Zoey found that she was enjoying herself as the crowds came to eat and drink and browse around the shop. Whenever she had a moment to spare, she stood in the doorway and watched the festivities.

There'd been no sign of Alex and she'd concluded that as someone of importance he was with the organ-

isers and those more interesting than the serving maids
in the post office.

The light was beginning to fade and winter's chill
settling on the street when someone came hurrying into
the shop to ask if they would phone for an ambulance.

'What's wrong?' she asked immediately.

'A youngster's fallen off the roundabout and hurt himself badly,' she was told.

As the postmistress began to make the necessary
phone call Zoey said urgently, 'Take me to him.'

The child was lying in a crumpled heap on the concrete beside the carousel. He wasn't moving, and as she
pushed her way past those gathered around him she
heard someone say, 'He's been riding on this thing all
afternoon. Must have felt dizzy.'

As she bent over him Zoey was relieved to see his
small chest rising and falling, but the gash on his head
and the subsequent swelling that was appearing around
it were not reassuring.

'Stand back, please,' she heard a familiar voice telling
the onlookers, and as if history were repeating itself Alex
was saying, 'I'll take over, if you don't mind. The
child's injuries are severe for such a short fall. I need to
check his pulse and that his tongue isn't—'

'I've already done that,' she said quietly, and as she
raised her head his jaw went slack. But he quickly re-
gained his composure and crouched down over the boy.

'We can't move him as there's no way of telling what
damage there is to the head,' Zoey continued. 'There
could be spinal injuries as well. Will someone ask the
folk at the shop for a blanket?' she cried. 'His body
temperature is dropping fast in this cold air.'

'Who was he with?' Alex asked of those standing
nearby.

'The kid was on his own,' the ashen-faced carousel owner told him. 'Came with a pocket full of coins and stayed on all afternoon.'

Someone came back with a blanket and soon they could hear the sirens of an approaching ambulance. 'I'm going with him. I'll stay until the parents arrive,' Zoey said quickly.

'Me, too,' Alex said briefly.

'How do you mean?'

'I'm coming, too.'

'What about your part in the proceedings here?'

'Done and dusted,' he said drily. 'I was only here to pull a switch.'

'Hadn't you better tell her ladyship?'

'Gloria? She's in the pub with the fire crew. She'll find out eventually.'

As the ambulance sped along the darkening roads Alex said in a low voice, 'Do me a favour, will you, Zoey?'

'What?'

'Take that thing off your head. I feel as if I've been catapulted into the middle of *David Copperfield* or something similar. I do like to be able to see your hair.'

If she hadn't been so worried about the boy she would have been laughing at the thought of what she looked like. The paramedic who was helping her to monitor the young accident victim smiled.

'I thought it was because you were a bit eccentric. I take it that you're the lad's parents.'

Alex shook his head.

'No. We're from the local fire station and were involved in the event.'

As they hung around Accident and Emergency while the boy was being examined, Zoey said flatly, 'Hospital visits seem to be the order of the day where you and I are concerned. It was like going back in time, having you bending over me and bossing the show.'

Alex was eyeing her questioningly.

'I'm not with you.'

'When we first met and the removal man had collapsed.'

'Oh, that. Yes. But on that occasion I soon found out that you knew what you were doing. At least with regard to that.'

'In other words, I make a mess of everything else.'

'If the cap fits.'

'Oh! You make me so angry!' she cried. 'Not a word about having Gloria swanning around beside you when you were doing the celebrity bit.'

'Grow up, Zoey,' he snapped. 'Do you really think that cuts any ice with me?'

At that moment there was a commotion beside the enquiry desk and it became clear that the parents of the injured child had turned up, both of them totally distraught at discovering what had happened.

'We were busy decorating,' the mother was wailing tearfully, 'and didn't know that Grandad had given George his pocket money. We thought that he was still around somewhere until...'

X-rays had shown that there was a subdural haematoma present in the skull and surgery would be required to stop the bleeding.

As Zoey and Alex left them to their own particular nightmare she thought dismally that nothing had changed between Alex and herself. It was still one step forward, two steps back.

*   *   *

It was Christmas Eve and the day of the wedding, but all the bright expectation Zoey had expected to feel was missing. She didn't have to look far for the reason. It lay with the man who lived in the house across the way.

But it was Mandy's day and she was determined that nothing was going to spoil that, so she prepared to put on an act for her sake.

The ceremony was at half past three and as the two women dressed themselves and the baby the immensity of the changes that were about to take place in her life began to hit the golden-haired bridesmaid.

This time spent with Mandy and Rosie had been the happiest time she'd ever known, she thought wistfully. She'd met Alex here, hadn't she? Alexander the Great! Strong, mesmeric…and unforgiving.

The sight of Mandy in her bridal outfit broke into her reverie and Zoey put aside her yearnings.

'You look lovely,' she breathed. 'Harry will be overcome at the sight of you.'

The bride-to-be smiled as she observed the slender figure in blue velvet, holding the smallest bridesmaid in one arm and a posy of white snowdrops in the other hand.

'You don't look so bad yourself. If a certain person doesn't melt when he sees you, I shall be most surprised.'

Zoey pulled a wry face.

'I wouldn't expect too much from that quarter if I were you.'

When Alex came across Zoey did some melting of her own. The grey suit and pristine white shirt he was wearing emphasised his dark attractiveness to such an extent that she felt her blood heat, even though he was observing her unsmilingly.

She wasn't to know that those dark, unreadable eyes were seeing a vision that was affecting him in a similar manner. In her long blue velvet dress, she was the loveliest thing he'd ever seen. So why was he being so unrelenting?

He wanted to take hold of her and kiss away the doubts in those beautiful eyes, but he wasn't here to make love to Zoey. Mandy had asked a favour of him and he'd been only too happy to oblige, even though the golden girl was going to be left out on a limb once her stepmother was married.

They were all going to the church together—Mandy, Zoey, the baby and himself. Harry would meet them there. Afterwards the four of them would sit down to the meal that had been arranged, with Rosie beside them in a high chair. Once they'd eaten, the bride and her new husband would set off for the honeymoon they'd planned, leaving Zoey to look after Rosie until they came back.

It would all seem a bit of an anticlimax once they'd gone, especially for Zoey, and he knew he wasn't going to be able to ignore her over the two days of Christmas. Every time he saw her he felt as if his very bones would melt with longing and knew that if he was fasting it was his own choice.

CHAPTER EIGHT

THE vows had been made, the knot tied. The wedding was over.

All the time the ceremony had been taking place Zoey had been remembering how Alex had found out about Mandy's light-hearted suggestion for a double wedding.

Was he recalling it, too, she wondered, and thinking he'd had a lucky escape from the local flibbertigibbet? That he'd made one mistake and wasn't going to make another in a hurry? It was because he wasn't in a hurry that everything kept going wrong, Zoe thought wryly.

They all went back to the house so that Mandy could change her clothes before she and Harry left for a short break in Spain. Now, just Zoey, Alex and the baby were left and, as if she sensed that her mother had left her, Rosie was becoming fretful.

Zoey was eyeing her in perplexity. She was usually such a good little soul that an unhappy Rosie was unheard of. But fretful she was, and Alex asked, 'Do you think she's sickening for something?'

She was trying to soothe her into sleep but Rosie wasn't to be coaxed and she said, 'It will be incredible if she is. It's the first time that Mandy has left her for anything other than a few hours.'

Alex was standing beside them, and as he looked down at her bent head tenderness washed over him. They were a beautiful sight, Zoey and the baby.

Rosie, blue-eyed like her big sister and with a golden

down on her small head, and Zoey, young and beautiful, watching over her like an anxious madonna.

'I have to go,' he said reluctantly. 'There are a couple of things I have to see to at the station before Christmas Day dawns, but I'll be back as soon as I can.'

'Thanks, Alex,' she said gratefully. 'I'm sure she'll be fine. I'll see you later.'

But as time passed, Rosie's temperature began to rise and she was far from well. Mandy always had infant paracetamol on hand and Zoey tried to coax the baby to take it, but it seemed difficult for Rosie to swallow and she tried to push the spoon away with a hot little hand.

Fearful of meningitis, Zoey lifted Rosie's vest, looking for the tell-tale rash that would be the forerunner to a nightmare. Thankfully the baby's skin was clear, and when Zoey shone a light in her eyes there was no increase in the discomfort.

Mandy and Harry would be somewhere in the sky at this moment, she thought, so she couldn't reach them if she wanted to, and she would have to be desperate to break into their brief time together.

The obvious thing to do was ring the GP, but she'd forgotten that it was the late afternoon of Christmas Eve and the only help available was a voice message giving details of the emergency service.

Rosie was coughing now, harsh, rasping noises that were quite frightening. It was going to have to be A and E at the nearest hospital, she decided, and hoped that the place wouldn't be full of those who'd drunk too much. Or people who'd slipped on icy pavements that hadn't thawed out from a drastic drop in temperature the night before.

Wrapping the baby up snugly, she ventured forth. As she pulled out of the drive she glanced quickly at the house across the way. It looked warm and welcoming, with an illuminated tree in the garden and coloured lights framing the porch. The curtains hadn't been drawn and she caught a glimpse of Gloria looking out, an unruffled figure with glass in hand, which made her gloom deepen.

There was no sign of Alex, but there wouldn't be. He'd said he had some work to do at the fire station before the day was out. Maybe the wedding had interfered with headquarters business and he'd gone to catch up. The place would be closed during the festivities but the men would all be on call if any major emergencies arose.

As Rosie's coughing broke into the silence, Zoey thought anxiously that she had an emergency of her own to cope with and hoped that he would find her somewhere along the way.

The casualty department of the hospital was as she'd expected it to be on Christmas Eve—full. But after the triage nurse had noted that Rosie was now having difficulty in breathing, they were seen almost immediately.

'It's a bad case of croup,' the doctor said. 'It's common in children under four and in most cases clears up when moist warmth is introduced into the atmosphere. Croup comes from a viral infection that affects the voice-box, the epiglottis that covers the larynx, and the trachea or windpipe. It seems to occur at this time of year for some reason and in the case of your little one we're going to have to hospitalise her so that she can be put inside a tent and given humidified oxygen.'

'I'm not her mother,' Zoey explained. 'Rosie is my half-sister. I'm looking after her while her mother is away.'

He nodded. 'I'll send for a nurse from the children's

ward to come and collect you,' he said, 'and one of the paediatricians will start the baby's treatment as soon as you're settled in there.'

Zoey had kept calm all through the crisis, but now that the treatment seemed to be working and Rosie was sleeping peacefully she was beginning to feel the after-effects.

It was just gone midnight. Seated in the dimly lit ward with the only sounds the restless stirrings of the small patients and the soft padding of the night nurse's rubber-soled shoes as she went to and fro, she felt isolated and exhausted.

For the first couple of hours she'd debated whether to get in touch with Mandy, but she didn't want to intrude into Mandy's honeymoon unless it was absolutely necessary.

Yet there'd been the dread of Rosie becoming worse and her mother not having been informed. Now, thankfully, that crisis was past. She might even be able to take the baby home in the morning. But it didn't take away the feeling of terrible aloneness.

Zoey could feel her eyelids drooping and knew that wouldn't do. She was there to watch over Rosie. It happened again and this time when she blinked them open she looked up, startled. She wasn't alone in the shadows. Alex was there, only inches away, his expression full of grave concern.

'Alex!' she breathed. 'How did you know where we were?'

'Simple deduction,' he said in a low voice. 'I was very late leaving the station because I discovered a burst pipe in the kitchen and had to rustle up a plumber, which is no mean feat on Christmas Eve, I can tell you. And when

I did eventually get away I saw that your place was in darkness.

'I naturally concluded that Rosie had improved and you'd gone to bed. Until Gloria said she'd seen you "gallivanting" off in the car earlier. I knew that couldn't be right. That you wouldn't leave the baby, even if she was well, and she was far from that the last time I'd seen her, so I decided to try the hospital…and here I am.'

He bent over the sleeping child.

'What was it?'

'A bad case of croup. Rosie is being given humidified oxygen as it's affected her larynx and trachea. She started to cough and it was dreadful. I've never heard anything like it. By the time we arrived here her breathing was affected and they saw to us immediately.'

'And?'

'It seems to be working. The doctor said if it didn't they might have to do a tracheostomy and I was frantic, trying to decide whether I should get in touch with Mandy or not.'

'But you didn't?'

'No.' There was a wobble in her voice. 'Do you think I did the right thing?'

'Yes. Now that she's improving. But I can see that it was no easy decision to make.'

'It was awful. The responsibility was immense. I felt so alone.'

She bent her head so that he wouldn't see tears on her lashes but she was forgetting that she was with a man who missed nothing.

'Come here,' he said gently, holding out his arms. 'You've had one heck of a night.' As she went into them like a homing pigeon, he went on, 'It's been some

Christmas Eve! You being worried sick over Rosie and ending up here and me chasing the plumber so that the station wouldn't be flooded.'

As she snuggled against him she could tell that he was smiling when he said, 'You're still in your bridesmaid's dress, I see. Couldn't you bear to take it off?'

She looked down blankly at the long folds of blue velvet.

'I haven't had a chance. Rosie was still in hers when I brought her here, but the nurse found her a little cotton baby suit.'

'So what happens next?' he asked.

'I don't know. It will depend on what the doctor says in the morning whether she's allowed home. If he's not happy to discharge her, I shall be here until he does. I can't believe that this has happened the moment her mother was out of sight.' Zoey sighed. 'What a nightmare.'

'You coped brilliantly, Zoey.'

She lifted her head to see his expression and as their eyes met she asked, 'So you don't think I'm the village nitwit after all?'

'I never did. I might have thought other things of you, but never that. You're strong and brave...and sometimes er...unpredictable and impatient. Shall we say that getting to know you is quite an experience.'

The night nurse was hovering and they stood back while she checked on Rosie.

'Her breathing is much better,' she told them, 'but I think the paediatric consultant might want to keep her in for another day, even though we are trying to keep the ward as empty as possible with it being Christmas.'

She smiled. 'So prepare yourselves for having Christmas lunch on the children's ward.'

'No problem,' Alex told her smoothly, and when Zoey eyed him in surprise he said, 'Well? Is there?'

'Not for me,' she agreed, 'but surely you'll want to be getting back.'

'What for? To watch Gloria spend the day beside a box of chocolates and a bottle of wine? I'll be where I want to be, so does that answer your question?'

It certainly did, Zoey thought as the night ticked away. Not so long ago she'd thought this was going to be the worst Christmas ever, but that wasn't how it was turning out. Rosie was getting better and incredibly Alex was here beside her and content to be so. If he thought that she was unpredictable, what was he?

The nurse had found them a couple of comfortable chairs and Zoey was dozing when Alex said suddenly, 'Were you disappointed that it wasn't a double wedding?'

Her eyes flew open. It was the last thing she'd expected him to say. She shook her head.

'No. The man I marry will have to be really sure that he wants to marry me. Not feel as if he's been rushed into something he might regret.'

'I take it that you are referring to me?'

'Mmm. Maybe.'

'And do you think the fact that I've been feeling rather disillusioned with you of late could have added to any doubts I might have? Especially as I've recently gone through a divorce?'

'It might have, I suppose,' she conceded. 'But you know how I feel about you.'

He raised a quizzical eyebrow.

'Do I? Should I be asking forgiveness for losing my cool when I saw you wrestling with Osbourne?'

'Exactly!' she exclaimed. 'Wrestling! Not romancing!

I was at a loose end when you cancelled our arrangements and he was there. But I didn't ask him to walk me home, or to start taking it for granted that I was going to be falling into his arms like a piece of putty.'

'That is a substance I would never liken you to,' he said laughingly. But he was serious again as he said, 'It will be daylight soon. The ward will be a hive of activity then. So while peace still reigns, merry Christmas, Zoey.'

As she observed him with her mouth a round 'O' of surprise, he put a small gift-wrapped box in her hand and told her, 'I wasn't sure if I would get the opportunity to give it to you, but the Fates had other ideas, didn't they?'

'Er...yes,' she said awkwardly, for once almost lost for words. 'Is it all right if I open it?'

'Of course. It is Christmas morning.'

She slowly unwrapped the gift to discover a bracelet of diamonds and sapphires. As she gasped with delight he said, 'Sapphires to match your eyes, and diamonds because they sparkle almost as brightly as you do.'

She held out a slender wrist for him to fasten it on and once it was in position she looked down at the glowing gems.

'It's beautiful,' she breathed, and getting to her feet she bent over and kissed him on the cheek.

He'd been right about her sparkle. It might have been missing of late, but now it was brighter than the diamonds as she told him, 'If we weren't here I would do better than that. But the children's ward is hardly the place to be kindling our desires, is it?'

Alex was smiling.

'You're assuming that the kindling would be mutual, then?'

'Wouldn't it?'

'It would depend,' he said with the smile still in place.

'On what?'

'Just how much will-power I was able to dredge up.'

At that moment there was an interruption. A porter, with anxious parents one on either side of him, was wheeling in a trolley with a sick child on it, and the moment was broken into.

'What about Gloria?' Zoey asked as a winter dawn streaked the sky.

'What about her?' Alex said smoothly.

'Won't she wonder where you are?'

'She knows that I went to find you.'

'And she didn't mind?'

'No, of course not. She's busy winding up her aunt's estate and then she'll be off.'

Gloria and her concerns seemed a long way off on this Christmas morning. Zoey said sleepily, 'We're like Mary and Joseph, watching over the child.'

Alex smiled. 'You've certainly got the blue dress on,' he quipped, 'and if I stay here much longer I'll have the beard that goes with the part.'

It was ten o'clock when the consultant came on his rounds, and when Zoey asked if Rosie could go home he shook his head.

'She's recovering satisfactorily,' he told her, 'but I'd like to keep her here under observation for another day at least. It was a bad attack. We nearly had to perform a tracheostomy, but fortunately the oxygen seems to be doing the trick instead.'

He turned to Alex.

'It's your wife that should go home. She looks exhausted.'

'I'm just a friend,' he said, 'but I agree with what you say.' He turned to Zoey. 'The doctor's right. You need some sleep. Rosie is in good hands. We can come back later.'

As she opened her mouth to protest he said, 'Shush. I'm taking you home. We'll come back after lunch.'

'What lunch?' she said wearily. 'All the food that Mandy bought is still in the freezer.'

He led her gently but purposefully out onto the hospital's main corridor.

'We'll call it breakfast, then. You don't keep your eggs and bacon or your cereal in the freezer, do you?'

'That's hardly what you would call festive fare. It's Christmas Day,' she protested weakly.

'So what? It will still have twenty-four hours in it. Become light, then go dark in the late afternoon, like any other day at this time of the year. At the risk of sounding trite, Christmas is where the heart is, not where the turkey's thawing out.'

Zoey had to smile even though she was drooping with tiredness.

'Very profound, I'm sure. But one can't eat pearls of wisdom, or thread them for that matter.'

'So what do you have in cereals?' he countered, ignoring the comment. 'Something other than cornflakes, I hope.'

This is fantastic, she thought as Alex tucked her into the car. We're friends again. Proper friends! We can laugh and joke together, and if we get back to doing other things together life will be great.

The promised breakfast didn't materialise. Zoey fell asleep in the car and when Alex awoke her at the other end the need for rest outweighed the need to eat.

She didn't undress, just flung herself onto the bed. The

last thing she remembered was Alex planting a kiss on her brow before he covered her with the duvet.

If she'd gone to sleep feeling cherished, she didn't waken up to the same feeling of contentment.

There was panic in her. Rosie! She'd left her at the hospital. What if she'd had a relapse or, confused by all the strange faces, was crying for her mother? She should never have let herself be persuaded to come home.

As the thoughts came crowding in, she found herself on her feet. Hair tousled, black smudges beneath her eyes, already back on the children's ward in her mind's eye. The turkey could stay in the freezer for ever.

'It's all right,' Alex's voice said from the open doorway. 'I've just phoned the hospital. Rosie has eaten all her lunch and after a quite lively time has gone back to sleep again, so there's no need to rush.'

She sank down onto the bed and looked at herself blearily. She was still wearing the blue dress, for goodness' sake! Alex had said that they needn't hurry back, so she was going to have a shower and then change into something else. If she never saw the dress again it wouldn't matter. It would always remind her of Rosie coughing and gasping for breath.

'You have to eat before you do anything else,' he said as if he were reading her mind. 'We have a nice line in muesli, porridge or fresh fruit. What would you like?'

Suddenly she felt light-hearted. She could relax. Rosie wasn't fretting and Alex was here, offering her a mundane menu that sounded mouth-watering when she thought about how hungry she was.

What had he said? Christmas was where the heart was. She'd given her heart to him, but what about his? He still wasn't committing himself to anything more than friendship.

When she went to eat the breakfast that he'd prepared, the turkey was glistening on the kitchen unit, looking as if it had just arrived from outer Siberia.

'If you like, I'll come over this evening and cook the meal while you're at the hospital,' he said. 'The bird should be thawed out by late afternoon, and if it isn't I'll use the microwave. You can decide then whether you just come back to eat and then return to the hospital for the night, or come back to stay if you think Rosie will be all right without you.'

'I don't deserve you,' Zoey said with a catch in her voice.

He smiled as he put a generous helping of bacon and eggs in front of her.

'You haven't got me yet.'

Her face sobered.

'Sorry. I keep forgetting that you don't want to be rushed.'

Alex's smile was still in place but his thoughts didn't match it. What was the matter with him, letting her think that? She was wearing the jewellery he'd bought her. Was thrilled with it. But he knew deep down that it should have been a ring. That was what he'd gone to buy. So why hadn't he? He knew that he wanted Zoey Lawrence in his arms, in his bed, in his life. So what was he waiting for?

When Zoey had finished eating she went up to shower and to rid herself of the blue dress, leaving Alex to clear away. After the lows of yesterday she was on a high. Thankful that Rosie was going to be all right and delighted that she had Alex all to herself for Christmas.

He hadn't been across to his own place since they'd

got back from the hospital, but she reckoned he would have to check up on Gloria sooner or later, and as far as she was concerned later would be fine.

She paused in the middle of towelling herself dry, viewing her nakedness in the bathroom mirror. At that moment she longed to feel his touch, his strength against her as they gave in to their need for each other.

But as far as she knew, Alex was still downstairs in the kitchen, clearing up after their impromptu Christmas breakfast. Making love to her would be the last thought in his head. With sudden recklessness she threw on a robe and ran downstairs, her bare feet making no sound.

He wasn't in the kitchen. All was neat and tidy, and as she hesitated in the doorway he asked from behind her, 'Are you looking for me?'

As she turned quickly the robe swung open, and with a bravado that was far from how she was really feeling she made no attempt to pull it together again.

'What are you trying to tell me?' he asked in a low voice. 'That you're beautiful, desirable…and available? I know all those things, Zoey. And I also know that if and when I make love to you, it won't be because you've made the first move. We're not Adam and Eve in the garden of Eden. It will be because we both want it more than anything else on earth.'

If the robe had been loose before, it wasn't now. She was pulling it so tightly around her it was cutting into her middle.

'Well, thanks for making that clear,' she said stonily. 'I hope that whenever you reach that state of bliss I'll be around to share it.' And on that note she marched back upstairs and got dressed.

When she went back downstairs Alex was reading a book, but he put it down when she came into the room.

'Could you drop me off at the hospital, please, Alex.' she asked. 'My car's still there.'

'All right. If you'll ring me when you know what time you'll be back to eat.'

'So you're still going to cook for us?'

'Why not? I said I would, didn't I?'

'I thought that you might have had enough of me and my crazy assumptions.'

He shook his head.

'I'm the one who's crazy.'

'You're just saying that to make me feel less rejected,' she said dolefully, 'and to make yourself seem not so cold and unfeeling.'

He was on his feet and moving towards her. 'So that's how you see me, is it?' he said with a purpose in him that was unmistakable.

Swinging her up into his arms, he began to climb the stairs.

'Put me down,' she gasped, her face scarlet with humiliation. 'You think I'm begging for it, don't you? Well, I'm not!'

He didn't answer. Just continued on his way up the staircase. When he laid her on the bed she gazed up at him in outrage for the briefest of moments and then she was rolling over to get out of his reach. He made no move to detain her and once she was on her feet allowed her to push past him as if she thought that the devil himself was about to ravish her.

She hadn't said a word all the way to the hospital, Alex thought with a wry smile on his face as he defrosted the turkey.

Zoey must be out of her mind if she believed he didn't want to make love to her, he told himself. When she'd shown him her nakedness it would have been so easy to have taken her there and then. To accept what she'd offered and worry about the implications afterwards. But he hadn't kept a hold on his desires for this long to have it end in swift lust. He was his own man. Not to be knowingly manipulated.

Just the same, there was no way he would have made love to her during those moments in the bedroom. Taking her up there had been merely a gesture brought about by her description of him.

When eventually they did make love it would be a joyous thing, combining passion, tenderness and respect, and he was prepared to wait until then.

He was still regretting not having bought the ring. But there was the New Year ahead of them with its hopes and aspirations. What better time for new beginnings?

And in the meantime he'd promised her a Christmas meal. Whether she would want to have anything to do with him after their little episode in the bedroom he didn't know. But if that did prove to be the case all she had to do was throw him out.

While the food was cooking he went across to his own house. Gloria wanted to know where he'd been.

'I was in the children's ward at the hospital for most of the night,' he informed her, 'and am now cooking a meal.'

'I see,' she said. 'So I'll be eating alone?'

He couldn't let her do that. Not on Christmas Day.

CHAPTER NINE

FOR the rest of the day Zoey put her own needs to one side and devoted herself to Rosie. The baby was no longer on the oxygen treatment and was sitting up and taking notice of all that was going on around her.

Some of the children in the ward were noisy and fretful and others, those who were really sick, were very quiet. There was sadness in Zoey as she watched them. Rosie's problem had been serious enough, but it was minor compared to what some of these young ones were coping with.

'When you take her home, keep the atmosphere warm and moist,' a staff nurse told her. 'It might sound odd, recommending a damp atmosphere, but that's what she needs for a day or two.'

She cast a sympathetic eye over the youthful figure by the cot.

'Not much of a Christmas you're having, is it? Being a parent isn't all sweetness and light.'

'I'm Rosie's half-sister,' Zoey explained. 'Her mother got married again yesterday and had only just left on her honeymoon when the baby became ill.'

'Have you told her?'

Zoey shook her head.

'No. I was very undecided, worried sick, in fact, but when Rosie began to improve I left it.'

'Where's your friend?' the nurse asked curiously, adding when Zoey eyed her questioningly, 'The guy you were with this morning.'

'I told him that he didn't need to come,' Zoey told her, thinking that 'friend' rather than 'lover' was an apt description of Alex's place in her life.

Yet she should be grateful for that, she supposed, as she had a feeling that those who had Alex Carradine for a friend were fortunate people. There was a strength and integrity about him that made other men seem insignificant.

Stop fretting over what's not on offer, she told herself, and make the most of what you've got. If he doesn't want to go to bed with you, at least he's making Christmas dinner. Just don't start thinking about which you would prefer.

She had Rosie on her knee and as the little one reached up and pressed a chubby fist against her face, Zoey said, 'You know what I want, don't you, little sister? So do I. It's just Alex who can't see the wood for the trees.'

It was six o'clock in the evening. The baby had been bathed and fed and was now sleeping soundly.

'Does she usually sleep through the night?' one of the nurses asked.

Zoey nodded.

'Then go home and enjoy what's left of Christmas Day. She'll be fine, and tomorrow it's almost certain that the doctor will discharge her.

'Go on,' she insisted as Zoey hesitated. 'We know where you are if we need you and, with the progress the baby is making, it's not likely that we will.'

Zoey's smile beamed out.

'All right. I will. I'll be back first thing in the morning.' And with a lighter heart than she'd had at the same time the day before, she went.

She was smiling as she drove home. Whatever dos and don'ts Alex had in mind, at least they were going to spend the evening together, shutting out the winter dark and relaxing in the cosy warmth of the house that her father had bought for his young wife.

Alex was at the stove when she went in and he immediately asked about Rosie.

'She's fine,' Zoey told him breezily.

'Good,' he said crisply, then said in a more subdued tone, 'Mandy rang to wish you a merry Christmas.'

She paused in the act of taking off her long winter coat.

'What did you say?'

'I'm afraid that I told her a whopper. I said you'd taken Rosie out in the pram for some fresh air and would ring her when you got back.'

'And what did she say to that?'

'To leave it until later as they were going out for a meal.'

'Phew! So we have a reprieve. Was she surprised that you answered the phone?'

'Not in the least. I explained that I was doing the cooking.' He paused and she was conscious of unease in him. 'And...er...with regard to that, I hope you don't mind, I've invited Gloria across. I can't leave her stuck there on her own on Christmas Day. She hasn't an awful lot going for her at the moment. It seemed the charitable thing to do.'

Zoey felt her brief lifting of spirits dwindle as she took in what he'd said. Once again his was the sweet voice of reason.

But it was the same old thing again, wasn't it? Keeping her at a distance. Safety in numbers. She was being unkind and knew it, but she couldn't help herself.

What on earth was she doing, pining for a man whose interest in her was so restrained?

'By all means,' she said coolly. 'Why not go out onto the highways and byways and see who else you can find?'

Alex was eyeing her sombrely.

'I knew that was how you would see it.'

'Yet you still did it.'

'If I think something is right, yes, I go ahead and do it. So, do I ring across and tell her to forget it?'

Zoey was already contrite, but wasn't going to let him see it.

'No, of course not,' she said blandly. 'She'll be able to chaperone us. Stop us from giving in to our animal desires...as if that were likely. I notice that you didn't try to stop me when I fought my way out of the bedroom.'

'Disappointed, were you?' he asked drily.

'No. I wasn't. I was more the nervous virgin,' she said with a toss of her head. 'But seriously, getting back to Gloria...'

'Yes?'

'It's been a strange Christmas all round. Sharing it with your ex-wife can't make it any more strange. It's fine by me for her to join us.'

'Good. My invitation to her stemmed from nothing more than a guilty conscience.'

'Why would that be, then?'

'Because I have so much. I have a job I enjoy immensely. I live in beautiful countryside and—' with a quizzical smile '—I've got you, babe.'

'Oh, no, you haven't...''babe'',' she hooted. 'You've passed up too many chances for that...and—' looking over his shoulder at the stove '—there's a pan about to boil over.'

As he went to adjust the flame she walked towards the door.

'I'm going upstairs to change and when I come down you can tell me what there is left to do.'

He waved his hand over the worktops.

'It's done…babe…and Gloria will be across shortly.'

Zoey smiled.

'Great! I can't wait.'

'Are you going to wear your bracelet?' he asked as she paused in the doorway.

Her mouth softened as she held out her arm.

'I haven't taken it off.'

'So I did manage to do something right?'

'Mmm. You did.'

It was on the tip of his tongue to tell her it should have been a ring, but that would have put to waste all the will-power he'd been hanging onto. So he just smiled and told her to get a move on as the meal was almost ready.

When she came downstairs a little later Zoey realised that the spectre at the feast had arrived. She could hear Gloria's flat tones coming from the sitting room and braced herself before entering.

'Hello, there,' Gloria said when she went in. 'Hope you don't mind me gatecrashing, but Alexander was so insistent.'

Zoey hid a smile. 'Alexander' was looking rather un-comfortable.

'No,' she said easily. 'Not at all.' And was surprised to find that she meant it. 'Christmas is not the time to be alone. Especially after a recent bereavement.'

For a moment the other woman looked disconcerted, but she rallied quickly enough and said, 'Yes, that is so.'

Alex looked away and Zoey thought, He's thinking I've done a quick about-turn. But, then, he already thinks I'm unpredictable.

Gloria was dressed in black from head to toe. She looked understated and elegant, and Zoey wondered if Alex would think she'd overdone it in her favourite dress of sapphire-coloured silk. One of her most treasured possessions, it matched her eyes and turned her silky bob into white gold.

Her glance met his and she knew she'd made the impact she'd desired. His gaze was telling her that she was beautiful and that would have been fine if they'd been alone and could have hopefully gone on from there.

She was beginning to feel deflated again. What she'd said to Gloria had been genuine enough, but the disappointment was still there. Would she and Alex ever be alone at the right moment...in the right surroundings?

As she ate the food that he'd cooked and drank the wine that he'd chilled, Zoey put on a show of good humour that had him glancing at her thoughtfully when he thought she wasn't looking.

For his own part, Alex was silent most of the time, leaving the two women to keep the conversation going. Zoey wondered if he was comparing them...the past and the present.

At last Gloria yawned and got to her feet. Zoey felt relief sweep over her. The ordeal was over. Maybe now she and Alex could... But his ex-wife was saying, 'I'm not too keen on going into the house on my own at this hour, Alex.'

It took Zoey all her time not to groan out loud as he responded, 'I'll come with you.'

When they'd gone she locked up and went wearily to bed. If Alex had said he was coming back she would have waited, but she wasn't a mind-reader. Certainly not where his was concerned.

It was proving to be a see-saw sort of Christmas, she thought, frustratedly punching the pillows on her bed. Up, down, up, down.

One of the ups had been getting through to Mandy during the evening and hearing that she and Harry were having a wonderful time. When she'd asked about Rosie, Zoey had felt able to tell her what had been happening now that the crisis was past and there was no more cause for alarm. But it hadn't stopped Mandy from saying anxiously that she would come home.

'There's no need, dearest,' Zoey soothed. 'Rosie is fine. I would have been on to you straight away if she'd got any worse, but she didn't. So enjoy your honeymoon.'

'I'm glad that you've got Alex around for moral support,' the anxious mother said.

Zoey found herself laughing.

'Oh, it's that all right.'

'What?'

'Moral.'

It was Mandy's turn to chuckle.

'So you're not making much progress with that gorgeous man.'

''Fraid not. I'm spending the evening with Alex and his ex.'

'Sounds delightful,' Mandy said, still amused.

'Tell me about it,' Zoey groaned, and after promising each other to speak again soon they said an affectionate farewell.

It was lovely to talk and Zoey felt better now that

Mandy knew about her small daughter's illness. It had been no problem telling her now, but Zoey shuddered at the thought of what it would have been like if she'd had to ask Mandy to come home because Rosie was in a critical condition. It had been on the cards, but thankfully the treatment had worked.

Sleep claimed her eventually and her last thought before it did was that she hoped that Alex's solicitations on Gloria's behalf weren't going to include anything further than the invitation to eat with them.

Alex had intended to go back. If only to make sure that Zoey wasn't too upset at having Gloria foisted upon her. He'd spent most of the evening in a state of longing for which he had only himself to blame. Yet he couldn't have left Gloria on her own on Christmas Day.

Every time he'd looked at Zoey he'd told himself that he was a fool to keep her in suspense. She was divine. Even at her most subdued she was like a bright beacon in his life, and what was he doing? Playing hard to get. As if he were the catch of the season. Once Gloria was safely inside he would go back and tell her all that was in his heart.

But he'd no sooner crossed the road than he turned to see that the house opposite was in darkness, and he thought ruefully that the message was clear enough. She wasn't expecting him to return.

Zoey brought Rosie home the following morning and might have been feeling more perky if it hadn't been for two things. They'd warned her at the hospital that the croup might recur, and she'd seen nothing of Alex since the night before.

Obviously he wasn't yearning for her company. The

whole affair was too one-sided, she decided glumly. Maybe she would ask for that transfer in the hope that out of sight would be out of mind.

Mandy was due back in two days' time and she still hadn't found anywhere to live. Obviously she and Harry wouldn't be rushing her, but it was only right and proper that she find somewhere.

She knew where she'd like to take up residence. In the slot that a certain brunette was occupying. But she was about to give up on that one.

And so Boxing Day dragged on, with Rosie's return being the only bright thing about it.

Alex phoned in the early evening and when Zoey heard his voice she sighed. She was about to bathe Rosie and took the call on a phone on the upstairs landing, holding the baby in one arm.

He'd had all day to phone. Why leave it until now? she wondered.

'What's the matter?' he asked when she answered. 'You sound rather distant.'

'I'm about to commence bathtime.'

'So? What's wrong? Do you want your back scrubbed?'

'You're living dangerously, aren't you?' She couldn't help but laugh. 'It's Rosie's bathtime that we're talking about.'

'Which answers my next question. I was about to ask if she was home.'

'Yes, she is, and she's fine, but they told me at the hospital that the croup may come back.'

'Just hope it doesn't,' he advised, and added, as if anxious to say his piece and be gone, 'I just wanted to check that you weren't too put out by having Gloria with us last night.'

'I can think of things I would have enjoyed more, but taking everything into account I suppose she served her purpose.'

'Meaning?'

'She kept us apart.'

'You think that's what I wanted?'

'Possibly.'

It was his turn to sigh.

'I'm not going to argue with you, Zoey, and in view of what you said about little miss about to have her bath, I'm going. But first let me ask, when are you back on duty?'

'Next Monday. I can't have any more time off. I've used up all my leave.'

'Right. So I'll see you when I get back. I'm going away for a few days.'

'Who with?' she asked before she could stop herself.

'No one. It's a course that headquarters have suddenly dreamed up out of the blue, and if I'm going to get the station officer's position it's sensible that I go on it.'

'Why didn't you tell me before?' she said listlessly.

'Because I've only just found out myself. There was a notification in the post that came on Christmas Eve and I've only just had a chance to open it.'

'I'll see you when you get back, then,' she told him, and in the silence that followed she replaced the receiver.

Her responsibility for Rosie was at an end. Mandy and Harry were back and looking extremely happy.

'I'm going to apply for a transfer back to the main station,' she told them on their first night home. 'I spoke to the station officer there before Christmas when the thought first came to me, and he said there should be no problem. As soon as it comes through I'll look for a flat in the city centre.'

Mandy was observing her anxiously.

'What about you and Alex?' she asked.

'It turned out to be just one of those things,' Zoey said lightly. 'It never got off the ground.'

'Are you sure?' Mandy persisted. 'He was here with you at Christmas.'

'Hmm. Briefly. But I haven't seen him since. In fact, he's away.'

'Not with that ex-wife of his, I hope.'

'No. He's gone alone.'

Mandy was like a dog with a bone.

'Where to?'

'On a course.'

On Sunday night she went to the pub. It was the first time she'd been out over the festive season. There'd been no signs of Alex so she'd concluded that he was still away and, that being so, she'd felt no urge to sally forth. But by the time Sunday had come she'd been getting restive.

She'd missed the men at the station while she'd been off. Their friendship and that of their wives and partners meant a lot to her and she would miss them even more when she transferred back to the city centre. The local station might be small in the vast organisation that was the fire service, but the staff's efficiency and camaraderie were second to none.

Zoey told them that she was thinking of moving back now that her stepmother had remarried. It wasn't the real reason but it would have to do. She wasn't going to tell them she was in love with Alex Carradine and that he wasn't doing anything about it.

There were cries of disappointment.

'You haven't been here five minutes,' Geoff said. 'Won't you change your mind?'

'Yes,' someone else cried. 'Don't leave, Zoey. You're one of us.' But she'd just smiled.

It was almost time to go when Alex came in and she wondered why she was considering torturing herself by leaving this place. How would she cope away from him?

He looked tired but perked up when he saw them and answered their questions about the course willingly enough. But his glance was on Zoey, standing on the edge of the group, struggling with her doubts and uncertainties.

She was getting ready to go when she found him beside her.

'How's the little rosebud?' he asked.

'She's fine, thank you,' she told him gravely, as her mind went back to the night they'd spent in the darkened ward, fraught with anxiety on the baby's behalf. 'And how are you? Did you enjoy the course?'

'Not particularly.'

'Why was that?'

'I just didn't want to be away at this time.'

'Why?'

'I thought you would know,' he said softly.

His eyes had darkened and she found that she was holding her breath, but before he could say anything else one of the men called across, 'Has Zoey told you she's leaving us?'

If he'd looked tired before, his jawline was as tight as a bowstring now.

'Is that correct?' he asked in a low voice.

'Yes,' she muttered. 'I'm thinking of moving back to where I came from.'

'And I'm the last to know?'

'You weren't around to tell.'

'And you couldn't wait?'

'You would have known tomorrow when I made a formal application to transfer.'

He took her to one side.

'Is it because of me, Zoey? Am I driving you away?'

'I don't want to talk about it.'

'Fair enough,' he said levelly. 'Let me have your transfer application and I'll send it to the appropriate department.'

He hadn't exactly tried to persuade her to change her mind, Zoey thought as she climbed the stairs to bed. Far from it. If she had been dithering at all, that had settled it. If Alex had told her he didn't want her to go, she would have stayed. It was as simple as that. But he hadn't, and that fact had a message of its own. He wasn't bothered.

It serves you right, she told herself. You rush into everything without giving it enough thought. You took it for granted that because you fell in love with Alex he would respond likewise, and he hasn't. You might have had your moments with him, but that's what they were, and moments don't make a lifetime's commitment.

He probably sees you as young and foolish, which is his mistake. But are you going to point that out to him? No! You've done enough of the running. Time to stop. Get on with your life.

It all sounded so sensible and definite when presented like that, but as she turned her face into the pillow it was misery rather than determination that was the uppermost feeling.

*   *   *

If Alex had been feeling low in spirits before, he was devastated now. If Zoey was leaving the crew so soon she couldn't have felt much empathy with the men and, with regard to her feelings for himself, she was soon giving up on them.

He'd come back aching to see her again and when she'd been in the pub his spirits had lifted immediately. It was always great to meet the rest of the crew outside working hours and when she was with them it was the icing on the cake.

But she'd had a knockout blow waiting for him. She'd asked for a transfer and that could mean only one thing. The romance that never had been was over. She'd given up on him, and who was to blame for that?

As he'd marched home with frustration churning inside him he'd known that no matter how much he hated the idea of her going, Zoey had to make up her own mind whether she was giving up on the rapport between them.

He smiled a grim smile. He'd like to bet it wasn't the word she would have used to describe their relationship. Phrases like 'one-sided affair' or 'playing hard to get' sprang to mind.

He supposed he should be grateful that she wouldn't be all that far away. They were only a few miles from the city centre. It wasn't as if the fire service had a station on the moon and she'd asked to be transferred there.

But the worrying thing was that there was a finality about what she was doing. As if she was shutting the door on an episode in her life that had turned out to be less than her expectations.

Gloria was in the lounge, watching television, but she took her eyes off the screen long enough to say, 'So you're back.'

He nodded. 'Yes, I'm back.'

'You don't look very happy.'

'I'm not,' he told her bluntly. 'Zoey has asked for a transfer.'

She got to her feet.

'I'm sorry about that. Maybe I can cheer you up.'

'Meaning?'

'Aunt Mary's affairs are settled. Sometimes it comes in handy, being a solicitor, and it's been a great help being on the spot instead of having to rely on correspondence. So I'm ready for off, Alex. I'm packed and will be out of your hair tomorrow.'

Her smile was wry.

'When I first came back I did wonder if we'd made a mistake and might get together again. But since then I've seen you with Zoey Lawrence and I know where your heart lies. Put what happened between us behind you, Alex, and go forward with my blessing.'

Gloria left early next morning and as Alex watched her car pull away from the front of the house, his feelings were a mixture of relief and sadness.

It was a great burden off his shoulders that she'd gone in the same frame of mind as before, with no rancour between them. He hoped that one day she might find the right person, as he had.

And that was where the sadness was coming from. He'd found Zoey and had let her slip through his fingers. Admittedly from the best of motives. But it was what he'd done nevertheless. If he started to plead with her to change her mind at this late stage, would he be influencing her against what was best for her in the long run? He wished he knew.

Sleeping in the house across the way was a woman

who was loving and totally unselfish, and he'd been keeping her at a distance for what were turning out to be ridiculous reasons.

Well, one problem was solved. Gloria had gone. Zoey would have no worries about her presence any more. But that didn't matter so much now. She was asking for a transfer because of him, not his ex-wife.

It was the day of New Year's Eve and the crew had already been out on two minor calls when a big 'shout' came through. A store in the city centre was on fire and all available fire crews were being asked to attend.

As they raced to climb aboard the engine Zoey was glad to be back. There was less time to think when she was working. When they weren't on a 'shout' there was the equipment to check, talks about fire safety to charity functions, and general station duties that they all took turns to do.

And now here was a big one. Made even bigger because it was a furniture store that was on fire in the midst of the crowds jostling each other in the after-Christmas sales.

Three fire-engines were already there when they arrived. Firemen from other stations were manning the hoses while others were helping people who were trapped in the upper storeys onto aerial ladder platforms.

Grim-faced policemen were keeping back the gaping public and asking them to disperse, but with no obvious effect, and as they pulled up alongside, a nearby church bell began to toll sonorously as if a harbinger of doom.

Zoey felt a shiver run down her spine and Alex's face was tense. This was a bad one. They could all see that.

'What's the score?' he asked of a fellow sub-officer.

'Suspected incendiary device,' he said tersely. 'We

think there could be others. The fellow who owns the store says there have been bad feelings between him and his ex-partner. That he's been threatened by him.'

Zoey took a deep breath. On one of the busiest shopping days of the year somebody wanted to blow up a furniture store.

'There are people trapped inside,' the man told them. 'The place was full when it went off. So your lot will be needed in there.'

'If danger has a taste to it, it's in my mouth,' Geoff said sombrely as they donned their breathing apparatus. 'Let's see if we can get some of these poor devils out.'

'The upper floors are cleared!' somebody shouted as they approached. 'Concentrate on the basement!'

As she groped her way down the stairs with Geoff and Alex in front, Alex turned and said, 'Think on Zoey. No heroics. Just do what you can, then get out.'

'Yes, boss,' she said levelly.

There were other things she wanted to say but it was neither the time nor the place. She wanted to tell him that tragedies like this made their own ups and downs seem as nothing, and that she wasn't going to give up on him.

'Over here!' came the call, and as they groped towards a smoking jumble of three-piece suites Zoey saw a mother and child lying unconscious on the floor. Close by was an elderly couple in a similar state.

'Take the child,' Alex commanded. 'We'll see to the others.'

Geoff had already hoisted the younger of the two women over his shoulder, and as Zoey picked up the child he pushed her in front of him.

'Get moving, Zoey, girl,' he grunted. 'Before there are any more explosions.'

And she did. Aware with a tight knot of anxiety around her heart as she staggered up the stairs that they'd left Alex in the basement with the old couple, and strong as he was he wouldn't be able to carry them both.

The moment she handed the child over to waiting paramedics she was back in there, dreading the sound of further explosions, but for the moment there was only the crackling of burning wood and rumblings…and smoke and flames more dense than before.

CHAPTER TEN

ALEX was coming up the stairs, carrying the old man, and when Zoey would have gone past him to get to the woman he shook his head and pointed over his shoulder.

As she peered through the smoke Zoey saw Greg bringing up the rear with the woman in his arms.

There seemed to be no sign of anyone else in that area. Other firefighters were at the other end of the basement and they were shouting the all-clear when there was another explosion that rocked the building.

It was either a fractured gas main or another incendiary, she thought frantically, and as Alex pushed on with his burden she saw that Greg and the old lady were buried beneath a pile of rubble that a few moments earlier had been a brick pillar.

There was silence where the shouts had been coming from and her heart sank. At that moment it looked as if she was the only one in there. So it was up to her to act fast before anything worse occurred.

But the flames were coming nearer. It was as if the air released by the second explosion had fanned them and Zoey could see that in a matter of minutes the whole area would be engulfed.

As she heaved the rubble off them she could see a hand with knotted veins sticking out. Then a scrawny leg appeared and she began to work even faster.

A moaning sound from under the bricks at the other side of the elderly victim told her Greg was alive, though for how long she didn't know. But she had grave doubts

175

about the inert figure that was still half-buried beneath the debris.

There was no pulse in the frail wrist, or heartbeat when she managed to find her chest, and the flames were like dancing dervishes coming ever nearer.

Zoey was flinging bricks and pieces of concrete off them with a strength she wouldn't have believed she possessed, and now Greg was visible. Mercifully he was conscious and she sent up a silent prayer.

'How badly hurt are you?' she gasped.

'My legs,' he groaned. 'I think they're broken.'

She was picking up the woman, desperate to try resuscitation but knowing there was no time.

'It's clear that we haven't been missed,' she told the injured firefighter. 'Try to drag yourself away from the flames, Greg, and I'll send help.'

Then she was off, staggering under the weight of her burden and dodging the flames as she went.

When Alex had deposited the elderly man into the care of ambulance personnel, he leant against the wall and took a deep breath. Thank goodness they'd got out of that lot before yet another explosion occurred.

Zoey and Greg had been right behind him so they must be somewhere around, and both of them feeling just as relieved as he that they'd made it out in time.

But when he'd got his breath back he saw that they weren't around…anywhere. He froze. Surely they weren't still in there? Zoey, his bright morning star, trapped in that inferno!

He'd known fear in his time. It went with the job, but never like this…the sick churning of terror.

'Two of my crew are missing,' he cried. 'I'm going back in.'

'Hold on!' somebody cried. 'There's one of 'em here now!'

As Zoey staggered into the light of day, carrying the body of the old lady, a cheer went up.

But there was no time for rejoicing.

'No pulse or heartbeat,' she croaked as the paramedics took over. Addressing Alex, who was as white as a sheet beneath the grime, she said, 'Greg's still in there, Alex. He's got leg fractures and goodness knows what else. He was trying to drag himself away from the flames when I left him.'

If she hadn't known him better she would have said Alex was traumatised, but it seemed that as usual his brain was working at top speed.

'Stay where you are,' he told her. To the others he cried, 'One of my men is still in there!' Then he disappeared into the smoke and flames. There was a surge forward amongst the firefighters. He didn't need to ask for volunteers. It was their job.

The old lady was dead. She'd been unconscious before being trapped in the rubble and hadn't stood a chance. Her husband, as yet unaware of her death, had fared better.

By the time Alex had passed him over to the paramedics, who were working with a team of doctors and nurses from the hospital, he was showing signs of recovery and had been taken to hospital. But he was still too much in shock to be told the sad tidings.

'His wife is the only casualty so far,' one of the policemen told her. 'Let's hope it stays that way.'

Zoey couldn't agree more. Her eyes were riveted on the burning building. Alex was inside there, along with other men who were prepared to risk their lives as part of the job.

They were strong, physically fit and kitted out for it, but there was always the dread that circumstances might prove too much for them.

The fire on the outside was under control now, but she knew that the basement, which was less accessible, was a different matter. Suppose there was yet another explosion?

Policemen were talking to the store's owner who was standing nearby with a look of such sick horror on his face that she thought grimly it would be a long time before he could forget what had stemmed from a disagreement, if that was what it had been.

Someone had passed her a mug of tea and as she sipped it slowly it felt as if her throat had seized up. Where were they amongst the rumblings and cracklings of the damaged building? she thought frantically. Had there been another fall of masonry?

When they came out, with Alex leading them and Greg on a stretcher, it was as if a huge weight had been lifted off her heart.

She wanted to hold him and never let him go again. Her love for him was in her eyes as she ran towards him. If she was transferred to the ends of the earth, nothing would ever change the way she felt.

But Alex was bending over Greg, his concern with the injured firefighter as they carried him to safety and the waiting hospital team.

When she appeared at Alex's side he said tersely, 'That was touch and go. Another few seconds and we would have lost him. It's a good job he was wearing the right gear and had the oxygen or he wouldn't have survived.'

Greg was conscious and he weakly caught at Zoey's arm.

'Zoey, I'm sorry for the way I behaved that night after the pub. I was so drunk—I really am sorry.'

Zoey regarded the contrite face of the injured man for a moment and then took his hand. 'Yes, you were drunk, but nothing really happened. You're forgiven, Greg. Just make sure you don't drink so much next time we're all out.'

Greg looked relieved and even managed a smile for her.

'Trust me to have to be rescued by action man,' he mumbled. 'I'd rather it had been you, blondie.'

'Next time I'll make sure it is,' she said with an answering smile.

'Promise?'

'Absolutely.'

She could sense Alex's relief in finding Greg able to talk coherently, but it didn't stop him from tutting impatiently and commenting, 'When you two have finished passing the time of day, this guy needs a different kind of attention from what he's getting now.'

Zoey managed a smile. If Greg was still able to flirt a little it showed that he was facing up to what had happened in his own way. Of course she knew he needed medical attention. She was the crew's trauma technician, for heaven's sake. But what had Alex expected her to do? Ignore the man's brave flippancy? Well, Greg wasn't the only one who could be flippant.

'Point taken,' she told him, 'but you'll have to excuse me. I always chat to men on stretchers.'

As the doctors took over he gave her a long level look. 'I'll leave you to it, then.' And went back to where the fire was trying to take hold again.

What exactly was he leaving her to? she wondered.

*   *   *

'That was a job well done,' Alex announced as they drove back to the station, minus Greg who was now hospitalised with two fractured femurs, a broken clavicle and minor burns.

They'd stayed to assist with the inspection of the premises once the fire had been brought under control, and it had looked as if they were dealing with arson.

'What sort of a person would blow up a building out of spite?' Geoff said incredulously.

'There are a few around, I'm afraid,' Alex told him. 'The police have been to his address but, needless to say, he wasn't there.'

He was still shaken from the horror of finding that Zoey had still been in the burning building, having believed that she'd followed him out. If anything had happened to her he would have had nothing to live for. To lose her would be like losing his life blood.

Gloria had told him to move forward, put the past behind him, and she'd been right. That was what he was going to do and not before time...if he hadn't left it too late.

Zoey had yet to discover that Gloria had gone. But if he told her, would she think it was a ploy to keep her with him, after all these weeks of trotting out excuses to hold her at arm's length?

Then, running true to form, he'd been snappy with her when she'd been talking to Greg. Letting the nightmare they'd just gone through make him less than understanding, when all she'd been doing was being her usual caring self. Not to mention the fact that Greg had confirmed Zoey's innocence that night he'd found them together. What was he like?

Those moments when he'd realised she hadn't followed him out of the building had been the worst of his life, and before he'd been able to tell her about his agony of mind there'd been the need to bring Greg to safety.

He could have told her then, when they'd been beside the stretcher. Yet what had he done? Pulled rank instead of joining in the brave banter of a badly injured member of his crew.

The day had gone by the time they docked the engine on the forecourt of the station and when Alex had made his report and checked that all was safe and sound before he and the others left, he found that Zoey had gone.

In a painful sort of way he was glad. At least while they were apart he wasn't likely to disenchant her further. It was New Year's Eve. The end of one year. The beginning of another. Whatever it held for them was in his hands.

Her transfer application was on his desk, waiting to go through. The coming days and months stretched ahead like a black abyss. Why didn't he tear it up?

When Zoey got home Mandy was setting the table for the evening meal and Rosie was in her high chair, playing with a plastic duck.

They both looked up and smiled when she walked in, and that did it. The scene was achingly tranquil. She was with those who loved her and suddenly it was all too much.

'That is it!' she exclaimed, flinging her bag down onto the nearest chair. 'I have had it with that man!'

Mandy looked up.

'I take it that we are talking about Alex Carradine?'

'Yes, we are,' she said wearily. 'Nothing I do is right for him. He is insensitive, snappy and—'

'You love him,' Mandy finished off for her.

'Yes, I do,' Zoey wailed, as the annoyance subsided.

'I can't believe what the two of you are like,' the other woman said. 'It's like missing the bus every time you run for it.'

'Yes, because the driver won't pick up any passengers that he thinks might cause him grief. He's not a chancer!'

'Can you blame him?' Mandy persisted gently. 'He has had Gloria for the last few years and is still being charitable towards her. If you want the man, do something about it. It's New Year's Eve, for goodness' sake. What better time to think of fresh beginnings?'

'I've done all I'm prepared to do,' Zoey told her. 'In fact, I've already accepted that it's over...not that it ever really began.'

'I never thought of you as someone who would give up so easily,' Mandy said chidingly, 'but if you aren't going to spend the last night of the old year with the man of your dreams, would you mind if I went to give Harry a lift to the pizzeria? We didn't want anything to stop you from spending it with Alex, but if you're not bothered I know he'd be glad of the help, as he's given time off to the people who staffed the place while we were on honeymoon over Christmas.'

'Of course go and help Harry,' Zoey said immediately. 'I'm going nowhere. I might stay up to watch the New Year in and that will be it.'

'You're too young and beautiful to be alone on New Year's Eve,' Mandy protested.

Zoey shook her head.

'Even if I wanted to go across the road, Alex has probably arranged to spend the evening with Gloria. He didn't want to leave her on her own on Christmas Day, and it will be the same tonight. So go and get ready.'

*   *   *

She had never known the house so quiet. Once Rosie had gone to sleep in cherubic innocence, a silence had settled over the rooms as if the whole place were waiting for something.

Zoey had switched the television on and off a few times, prowled around the lounge looking for something to read, and had finally ended up staring into space.

She had no yearning to be out there with the merry-making crowds if she couldn't be with the one person who mattered.

You ought to be making resolutions for the coming year, she told herself as she stared into the glowing coals of the fire. But with the shambles that was her present state of mind, she felt it would take her all her time to decide whether to get up in the mornings, let alone start mapping out the year ahead.

She'd been to the window a few times and gazed bleakly at the house across the way. All the lights were on so someone was still in there. Maybe it was Gloria, and Alex was out partying somewhere. That thought brought no cheer with it.

As the night wore on she weakened. If he was over there, the least she could do was wish him a happy new year. Surely he wouldn't read anything provocative into that.

At five minutes to twelve she checked on Rosie and went to find a coat. If Alex wasn't there, her absence would be only seconds. If he was, it still wouldn't be much longer than that if what had happened earlier in the day was anything to go by.

Alex had seen Mandy's car drive off, which meant that Zoey and the baby were alone in the house, as it stood to reason that the new husband would be at his restaurant. Why was she in there, though? Surely she wasn't going to stay in on New Year's Eve, even if it only meant going to the pub.

But the evening wore on and Mandy didn't come back. Finally it dawned on him that she must be helping her husband at the pizza parlour.

So Zoey had been left with the baby again. It seemed a bit unfair. But he knew how she loved the child. If she was like that with Rosie, what would she be like with a baby of her own...theirs?

His smile was wry. He'd handled it so that the chances of that were remote. He could count the number of times he'd kissed her on one hand, let alone made love to her. He'd let ridiculous concerns detract him from what really mattered and had been so determined that he wasn't going to make the same mistake twice that he'd fallen over backwards to keep his blonde enchantress in her place.

He looked at the clock. Ten minutes to twelve. He couldn't let the old year go out without telling her how much he loved her.

As Zoey lifted her hand to open her front door, the bell rang. When she opened it Alex was there in the porch. She felt her heart jolt in her breast, but her greeting gave no sign of it.

'Yes?'

He smiled.

'Can I come in?'

She stepped back without speaking.

'Where were you off to?' he asked, observing that she had her coat on.

Swallowing hard, she said the first thing that came into her head.

'I was going to feed the birds.'

'Seems a funny time to think of doing that.'

'Er…yes…maybe it is. There was some bread left over from the meal and I thought…' Her voice trailed away when she saw the amusement in his eyes. Determined not to be undermined, she said stiffly, 'So what can I do for you, Alex?'

'You can tell me that you'll marry me.'

'Wha-at?'

'I love you, Zoey. I always have from the moment I saw you, but I kept trying to convince myself that the timing wasn't right. As if that mattered.'

She was gripping the back of a chair for support, her wide blue gaze full of amazement.

'Why the change of mind?' she breathed. 'It's taken you so long!'

'It's not a change of mind. More an acceptance of what's been in it ever since we met. Please, tell me that I haven't messed things up completely. That your feelings for me haven't changed.'

'They won't ever do that, Alex,' she told him with a sweet gravity that made his bones melt. 'What I feel for you is deep and true, not just a girlish crush. I want to give you babies, spend every second I can with you, if you'll let me.'

'Oh!' he groaned. 'I'll let you! If you only knew the number of times I've wanted to put every other thought to one side and accept that I love you.'

She was still clutching the chairback and he smiled.

'Wouldn't you rather hold onto me?'

'Every day and always.' She beamed.

'So come on then, Zoey, darling. Let me show you

how much I really care.' And this time as she went into
his arms there were no doubts, no uncertainties, just joy-
ful amazement that what she'd longed for was going to
be hers.

Later, Zoey asked, 'What do you think Gloria is going
to say about this?'

'Gloria has gone,' he said drily. 'She finally sorted
out her aunt's affairs and had no further reason to stay.
She accepted that I was head over heels in love with you
and actually told me to do something about it. So it
would seem that we have her blessing.'

'Oh, Alex!' Zoey breathed. 'And I thought that she
wanted you back.'

'It might have been like that when she first appeared,
but after she'd seen what you mean to me she was happy
to bow out gracefully.'

'We'll invite her to the wedding,' she vowed.

He laughed.

'If that's what you want. The way ahead for us is
crystal clear now, my darling. I'm the one who's been
muddying it up, but not any more. It's going to be you
and I putting out fires, until the time comes for you to
produce those babies that you've promised me. And as
to the flame that we have kindled between us, it will
burn more brightly with every moment we're together.'

Rosie was a bridesmaid again, but this time she was
making her progress down the aisle in her mother's arms
and it was a different bride, a different groom.

When the ceremony was over there was something
else that was different. The sight of it made her wriggle
excitedly in her mother's arms.

The traditional wedding car had been replaced with a
big red fire-engine, and as the beautiful bride and her

new husband climbed aboard they were cheered on their way by men in funny coats and big yellow hats.

Rosie didn't know what it was all about, but maybe one day her big sister would tell her.

Modern Romance™
...seduction and
passion guaranteed

Tender Romance™
...love affairs that
last a lifetime

Sensual Romance™
...sassy, sexy and
seductive

Blaze Romance™
...the temperature's
rising

Medical Romance™
...medical drama on
the pulse

Historical Romance™
...rich, vivid and
passionate

27 new titles every month.

*With all kinds of Romance for
every kind of mood...*

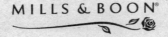

MILLS & BOON®

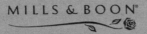

MILLS & BOON®

Medical Romance™

DEAR DOCTOR by *Meredith Webber*

Kirsten is engaged – sort of – to handsome rancher
Grant. So what if playboy paediatrician Josh Phillips
broke her heart? She's over it – and over him.
Kirsten wants commitment, the one thing Josh can't
give her. So why has her engagement done nothing at
all for Kirsten's heart...and punched a hole in Josh's?

SURGEON ON CALL by *Alison Roberts*

Joe Petersen is a skilled surgeon – unfortunately,
when it comes to being a dad he's a complete
amateur! Joe's working with emergency consultant
Fliss Munroe, and he wants her to be more than a
colleague. What better way to get her interest than
to recruit her to plan the best ever birthday party for
a five-year-old girl!

THE DOCTOR'S ADOPTION WISH
by *Gill Sanderson*

When Nurse Jane Hall returns from California to
help Dr Cal Mitchell take care of their orphaned
niece, his life, his plans and his emotions are thrown
into disarray. Jane might be a wanderer at heart,
but Keldale is her home – and if Cal could only admit
that he's fallen in love with her she just might stay
for ever...

On sale 7th February 2003

*Available at most branches of WH Smith,
Tesco, Martins, Borders, Eason, Sainsbury's
and all good paperback bookshops.* 0103/03a

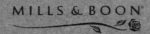

Medical Romance™

DR MICHAELIS'S SECRET *by Margaret Barker*

An emergency rescue on Ceres Island has recent arrival Staff Nurse Sara Metcalfe working with local doctor Michaelis Stangos – and from the moment she sees him diving into the waves she's hooked. But Sarah senses he's hiding a painful secret. A secret that's holding him back from what could be a perfect relationship...

THE FAMILY PRACTITIONER *by Leah Martyn*

Life is pretty uneventful for Joanne, working at the local clinic – until her teenage son Jason comes home with an outrageous request that sends Joanna marching off to see just what Dr Matthew McKellar is up to! Suddenly her life is in chaos. She's got a new job, with Matt as her new boss – and as her new lover...

HER CONSULTANT BOSS *by Joanna Neil*

Dr Megan Llewellyn couldn't work out what she felt most for her boss, consultant Sam Benedict – exasperation or desire! Was he hiding an attraction to her that was as intense as hers for him? When a fire destroyed her home and Megan found herself living with Sam she quickly found her answer!

On sale 7th February 2003

2 FREE

books and a surprise gift!

We would like to take this opportunity to thank you for reading this Mills & Boon® book by offering you the chance to take TWO more specially selected titles from the Medical Romance™ series absolutely FREE! We're also making this offer to introduce you to the benefits of the Reader Service™—

- ★ FREE home delivery
- ★ FREE gifts and competitions
- ★ FREE monthly Newsletter
- ★ Exclusive Reader Service discount
- ★ Books available before they're in the shops

Accepting these FREE books and gift places you under no obligation to buy, you may cancel at any time, even after receiving your free shipment. Simply complete your details below and return the entire page to the address below. *You don't even need a stamp!*

YES! Please send me 2 free Medical Romance books and a surprise gift. I understand that unless you hear from me, I will receive 4 superb new titles every month for just £2.55 each, postage and packing free. I am under no obligation to purchase any books and may cancel my subscription at any time. The free books and gift will be mine to keep in any case.

M3ZEA

Ms/Mrs/Miss/Mr ....Initials................................
BLOCK CAPITALS PLEASE

Surname ....

Address ....

....

....Postcode...................................

Send this whole page to:
UK: FREEPOST CN81, Croydon, CR9 3WZ
EIRE: PO Box 4546, Kilcock, County Kildare (stamp required)